THE FINAL STEP

LOC

LIKE

AND

KY

THE FINAL STEP

BY
RIDLEY
PEARSON

HARPER
An Imprint of HarperCollinsPublishers

Library of Congress Control Number: 2018939232
ISBN 978-0-06-239907-6

Typography by Joe Merkel
18 19 20 21 22 PC/LSCH 10 9 8 7 6 5 4 3 2 1
❖
First Edition

*In Memory of Zackery Kendall Luff, who
loved Shakespeare, lived like Michelangelo,
and never looked back.*

Dearest Reader,

The following is as best I can remember it. I've used a variety of sources to re-create the events. When I wasn't actually in the room, I've interviewed witnesses who were. I've studied texts, photos, and my brother's writings in his diary. Harder than tracking the events was keeping my emotions out of the passage. It's my brother, you see. My once sweet, loving brother who went from my best friend to something of a stranger. I'd never experienced anything like it.

Our mother left us when we were young. Our father died recently, leaving us orphans and in the care of our former nanny. Yes, our family was wealthy, but we were never rich. Rich is a whole family, and that's nowhere in my or my brother's memory.

I didn't want to tell this story. It's not easy to lose your best friend. But I owe an explanation to all concerned. Read at your own risk.

MORIA MORIARTY

CHAPTER 1

The sound cracked the night like a distant limb tearing from a tree trunk. It briefly put a halt to the riotous complaint of the cicadas, crickets, and bullfrogs. The forest canopy, thick with leaves, blotted out the ambient light from the stars.

James Moriarty, huddled in no-man's-land with two of his summer school classmates, Maverick Maletta and Ryan Eisenower, snapped his head up with the sound.

"That sounded like a gunshot," Eisenower said. Big and thick, even for fifteen (he'd stayed back a year—twice—in middle school), Eisenower had the voice of a man, the buzz-cut head of a sailor, and the chin of a boxer.

"Ryan," Maverick said, "you really think people are shooting at each other in a game of capture the flag? Seriously?"

"It was a firecracker. Maybe a distraction," James said, his eyes shifting as he calculated. "Did you hear it echo? It came from way over there somewhere. It's perfect for us. We can use it. We should attack now. At most, they've got two or three guys on this side of their defense. You two sweep in at a full sprint. They'll go after you. I will delay and come in behind. If they catch you, I'll free you. The three of us get the flag and get back."

The field of play, marked by battery-generated red-flashing roadside emergency lights, was a big chunk of forest and meadow on a bench of the hill leading from the main campus down to Baskerville Academy's hockey rink. No-man's-land divided the teams' territories. At either end hung a flag. Half the summer school had signed up to play. It was a lot of forest to defend for both teams, making the game all the more electrifying. Two teachers were supervising, one at each flag.

"You're saying we're the sacrificial lambs," Maverick said.

"Something like that," James replied, laughing.

"Works for me," said Maverick. He checked with Eisenower, who nodded and grunted.

"So, what are you standing here for?" James asked, prodding.

The boys took off, crossing the no-man's-land boundary and entering into enemy territory.

James began counting to thirty.

CHAPTER 2

TEAM BLACK HAD MORE ATHLETES THAN WE did. More speed. Probably more dumb nerve. The other Red girls and I—nine of us—had powwowed briefly. We agreed not to come off as girly or timid. We would not be afraid of the dark. We would not shriek at the first breaking of a twig. We would, in essence, "man up," the irony of which was not lost on any of us.

My brother, James, was on Team Black. That complicated things for me. For one thing, I knew how sneaky he could be. We had spent our childhoods playing two-person hide-and-seek. For another, he was devious, mean, cruel, and fun. A brother. Most of all, he was devilishly smart. If he got control of Team Black he would make a plan that the Reds could not beat. Thankfully, he wasn't all that popular. He had a group of goons he bossed around, but I think the other students saw him as a loner. Our great-great-grandfather had started Baskerville Academy, meaning most of the kids at school believed James and I got special treatment. It wasn't entirely true, but when did truth matter in high school?

Team Red's strategy, dictated by our team captain—a boy, naturally—involved putting more of our team on defense at the start of the ninety-minute game. I didn't say anything—no one would listen anyway—but it was a good strategy. James was aggressive. He would be thinking offense.

We Reds would focus on putting as many of their team in jail as possible. (Those in jail had to be tagged by a free teammate to win release and could not try for the flag until crossing back into no-man's-land first.) When we had ten of Team Black in our jail, the plan was to shift our resources to offense.

As a result, over twenty-five out of the thirty

Reds were assigned to patrol a grid space on our side of no-man's-land. We each had a lot of ground to cover.

We had agreed on code words to help signal each other.

"Charge!" I heard a fellow Red announce. As long as the attack did not intrude into my zone, I was under orders to stay within my area. I heard the breaking of sticks, the whipping of leaves, the rake of feet flying across the leaf-strewn forest floor. Two, three, four, or more at once. I held my ground, as agreed.

Ten yards in front of me, a crack of a twig. I posed, stock-still, with my arms away from my body in an attempt to appear more treelike. The forest was painfully dark. My eyes saw only blobs of purple and black among the inkish columns of tree trunks. Pinpointing the source of a sound was tricky given the occasional granite boulder and dozens of trees surrounding me. I waited.

The moving shape that appeared from the gloom was that of a boy darting from one tree to the next. He utilized a zigzag pattern, his silhouette pausing to blend into the tree trunks.

I held my breath as he came within five yards of me.

"You," I said. It wasn't a question.

"Moria?"

"Brother Bear."

"I'm faster than you."

"So you think," I said. "You going to test it, James?" He was the endurance runner. A sprinter, I could catch him before no-man's-land.

"Do I have a choice?"

"I'll pretend to chase you back to no-man's-land," I offered. "Next time you cross, stay out of my zone."

"You'd do that?"

"What are sisters for?"

"I've wondered that for a long time."

Someone set off a firecracker. That would not go down well with our chaperones.

"Now or never, Jamie. No more chitchat."

He took off. I followed, close enough to where I knew I'd tag him if he tried to burn me. I stopped twenty yards short of the no-man's-land line and watched him disappear across the rough dividing line.

As I made my way back to my zone, I heard the shout of "redcoat" twice from deep within our territory. We'd taken two prisoners. A few minutes later, the same code word was shouted three more times. Five total. Ten minutes later we had seven in our jail. It seemed our strategy was paying off. I kept to my zone, patrolling on tiptoe, making sure I covered all my allotted ground. On this warm summer night, I was sweating more from nerves than temperature. I didn't like the dark. I rounded a tree and recoiled from a face full of spiderweb, tipping forward and brushing out my hair and dry-washing my face to remove any chance of a spider crawling on me. I shivered, all raw nerves.

Twenty minutes into the game, we'd taken eleven of Team Black as prisoners. Those of us on Team Red designated as offense were expected to move toward no-man's-land, me among them. I found my way into a vacant stretch and quietly searched for my teammates. I gave up when I realized I had happened upon an abandoned lane into enemy territory. I had an obligation to my team to explore.

The move to offense filled me with a needling static. My skin prickled. My heart sped up. I marveled not only at the changes, but their cause, the switch from protective to vulnerable. My earlier experience told me it was a game of sound. Not running speed. Not even strategy. Sound. In this kind of darkness, the quietest team would win—of this I felt certain. Moving with great care, toe-to-heel, I pretended I was walking across a freshly iced pond, uncertain if the ice would hold me. With patience as my ally, I used all of a twelve-year-old little sister's guile and fortitude to withstand the temptation to hurry. Let others hurry, I told myself. I was in this to outsmart and win. James and I had played countless games of hide-and-seek, whether in our Boston townhouse or the Cape Cod compound, both of which had been left to us following our father's fatal fall from a stepladder. I knew all about staying put, holding my breath, and outlasting my brother's intemperance.

Fifteen minutes passed. I'd made it less than twenty yards. But there was close to an hour left of playing time; I wasn't in any rush.

Pretty soon, I reached a break in the forest where it gave way to a small meadow of knee-high grass and bunches of gnarly thornbush. I hesitated at the meadow's edge, considering circumnavigating it to avoid being seen. The meadow basked in starlight that the forest did not. Calculating the time it would take to go around, I elected to risk the crossing, but on hands and knees.

I'd not worn shorts the way others had. Despite the heat, I was in jeans to protect against the underbrush. With the Midsummer Dance quickly approaching, I didn't want to show off gashed legs and scabs. I crept forward slowly, sensing I was being watched.

Before I could decide on a plan, an anguished cry echoed across the field. It was not a call of peril. Not a call for help. It was the sound of something done and unchangeable. Something tragic.

I wanted to think of it as part of our game, a squeal of defeat or surprise. But it came from someone older than anyone on Team Black or Red. Not bigger, as some of the teen boys playing were, but seasoned. A voice that knew enough to try not to be heard. I wanted to turn back. I longed for no-man's-land.

A shadowy figure stepped out from behind a tree ahead. Suddenly my feet wouldn't move. I felt as if I might pee myself. The shadow dissolved in the starlight. A boy appeared.

James.

CHAPTER 3

"I THOUGHT I WAS BEING WATCHED," I SAID, MY pulse restarting, my breathing returned. "You owe me one. Lucky me!"

I knew my brother's body language. I instantly understood my mistake: Never trust James. He was not going to play fair. He was going to attack. He was going to capture me.

I was saved by blind luck: As he charged for me, James tripped and fell. It wasn't a stumble. It was a face plant.

I took off like an Olympic sprinter. I watched for trees, thickets, and rocks. But I was a scaredy-cat in panic mode and I glanced back. I ran straight into a tree.

Off-balance, I grabbed for anything to keep me from falling.

I grabbed for what felt like a branch.

But it was . . . warm.

Not a branch. An arm.

Not a kid, but a man wearing a sport coat.

My grip slipped or I missed. I tore off a button as I fell.

And from the ground, I looked up into his face.

He wasn't any of the grown-ups at Baskerville.

CHAPTER 4

Fear owned me.

I couldn't get a breath. I didn't want to look into his face again. I wanted to vanish into thin air. I looked away.

I heard a *thump*. The man groaned and staggered. A small stone fell into my lap and spilled into the leaves at my feet. He'd been beaned with the rock. James! I thought. My Brother Bear the savior.

I wasn't about to strike up a conversation. I rolled, came to my feet, and ran. Team Red didn't have any alarm codes for adults crashing our game of capture the flag. And even still, my throat was too tight to scream.

No idea why I thought about the rock, but I did. It was too small to have been thrown from a distance. And James was not the boy to carry around a slingshot. So who had saved me, and why?

My voice burbled back up. "Red dog!" I tried to shout. It came out "Ed hog" or "bed log." Like I was choking. Definitely not "red dog."

I broke into a clearing. I saw five kids standing next to the flag. It hung from a low tree branch and was lit by a flashlight. Prisoners! My Team Red teammates! I spotted two Team Black guards as well as a solo defender of the flag. (By rule, the defender had to stand outside a fat white circle on the ground.)

Two of my teammates appeared, responding to my earlier alert. We matched the defensive team in numbers. There were rules concerning freed prisoners. Our team had discussed how to deal with this situation. Given the even numbers, we had a real shot at winning the flag.

For a moment, I'd nearly forgotten about the man in the suit.

Nearly, but not really.

CHAPTER 5

In any other game, James would have gotten up and come crashing after me.

But he was, instead, on all fours next to the
thing that had tripped him. It wasn't a log. It wasn't
a rock. It was a leg. A man's leg. A man attempting
to crawl.

As I had broken away from the dazed man in
the suit, James had stayed still on the ground to
avoid being seen. He'd heard the stone whiz overhead; had heard it thunk and a man's voice groan.
A teacher? Whoever had beaned a teacher was
going to get it!

But why would two teachers be in the woods in the middle of capture the flag? Made no sense. He stayed low as the man hit by the stone lumbered off.

By this point, James could see the face of the man he'd tripped over, who was dragging himself across the grass.

"Mr. Lowry?" James rose to his knees. Not a teacher. The family lawyer. Out here, in the middle of the forest, a long way from Boston, where he lived and worked. "Are you okay? What are you doing here?"

James saw a large, oddly-shaped stain on Lowry's suit coat. How'd he get wet out here? He touched it. Sticky, not wet. Blood, not water.

"What's going on? Are you all right?" It was a stupid thing to say given the man's position on the ground and the size of the blood stain. A better question might have been: "How are you possibly still alive?" James spotted a tiny dark circle inside the stain. "You've been . . . *shot*!" He tried to roll the man, but Lowry groaned, reached out, and stopped him. "It's James, sir."

"James?"

"Moriarty. Yes, sir."

Lowry grabbed James by the shirt. It happened so fast, it frightened James. *"Elves and the*

Shoemaker, James. Elves and shoemaker. Repeat it." Lowry's legs were twitching. He looked like a guy trying to take his shoes off without unlacing them.

"James?" The man's voice had jumped an octave.

It wasn't Lowry. It took James a second to recognize the new voice as Lexie Carlisle's. He and Lexie had issues. They'd been a little closer than just friends in ninth grade. Things hadn't worked out so great.

"Lexie?"

"Who *is* that on the ground?" She came out of the dark. The clearing offered starlight.

"Say it," Lowry demanded of James.

"Elves," James said.

"And?" said Lowry.

"Elves and the Shoemaker," James said.

"Take it," Lowry said. He pushed his right shoe all the way off.

Lexie kneeled alongside James. "He's hurt."

"You think?" James said.

"Shut up."

"Take the shoe," repeated Lowry.

"James?" Lexie said.

"It's Mr. Lowry. You know, Father's lawyer."

"But . . . What's he doing *here*?" She inhaled

loudly. "James! You didn't—"

"What? Me? Come on, Lexie! Seriously? I found him like this. Just now. Right here. There was this other guy. And Moria. Over there."

"Moria? Where?"

"She took off. The guy . . . I didn't see."

"I'm calling nine-one-one!" Lexie said, yanking her phone from her back pocket.

Lowry's hand swatted it onto the ground. Lexie screamed loudly.

"Shh!" James chided.

"No ambulance," Lowry said. "No time."

"We've got to get help!" James said. "Call them!" he told Lexie.

"No!" Lowry yanked Lexie's wrist.

"You can't involve the *school*, James. The school's legacy. Think!"

Lowry was speaking in code to James. He was protecting the Scowerers, a secret society. A criminal society. James had been initiated as a Scowerer following Father's death. He now headed a secret criminal society hidden in the secret chamber beneath Baskerville Academy.

The police were unwanted. By talking about legacy, Lowry had made sure Lexie wouldn't understand. Lowry being shot involved the Scowerers.

"Headmaster." Lowry coughed wetly.

James was glad he couldn't see all that much.

"I'll get Crudgeon!" Lexie said.

"No!" both James and Lowry said together.

Lexie, balanced on her haunches, fell back with the rebuke.

"We'll both go," James said, taking the man's discarded shoe in hand.

"We can't leave him!" Lexie said.

"You have to," Lowry said, coughing blood. "They'll come for me."

"Who?" James asked sharply. "Who did this? Mr. Lowry? Who?"

The air was still. Lowry silent and unmoving.

"I think he's . . ." James couldn't get the word out.

James and Lexie snapped their heads around as something heavy moved through the forest toward them.

"James?" she whispered.

"I think he . . . I d-don't think he's b-breathing," James said, stuttering.

The short distance between James and Lexie seemed to shrink in the darkness. The sounds of breaking of sticks and the clomping of feet marched toward them.

"This way!" Lexie said, pulling James with her.

CHAPTER 6

I'D COME TO LOVE THE SCHOOL'S DARKROOM.
Digital and old-school photography occupied one
small area in the school's makerspace. I was old
school: it was chemicals, racks, dryers, and projectors for me. At first, the smell of the chemicals made
it unpleasant. The eerie red light felt spooky and
threatening. And then there were the photos themselves, black-and-white images clipped to wires
and hanging down like flags: faces, places, and
such. The darkroom was intense. I had to focus on
ratios, timing, science. I liked shooting old-school
film, as our teacher had us doing our first year.

Digital photography would follow next semester, but the idea was that knowing where photography had started, learning how to take a strip of film and make pictures, gave the form meaning. I was hooked. I spent whatever free time I had developing film and making prints.

Focusing on my darkroom work also served as an escape from my thoughts. It was nice to find a place where I could get into a zone that pushed away roommates, my brother, my studies, the pressures that came from living and playing with other boys and girls. In the darkroom I entered the world of image, leaving the world of personality behind.

This "zone" was something new to me. I'd heard people talk about it: musicians mostly. I'd never experienced it for myself except when reading— being so immersed in, so part of something I forgot I was breathing. Once into the darkroom I forgot basically everything but the roll of film or the photograph I was developing.

I forgot to lock the door.

Locking the door was critical to preserving your film and prints because an open door meant light and calling it a darkroom was not just a cute name. If the room wasn't dark, the work was ruined.

The door came open, and with it light. My pictures were toast! I turned to confront the moron who hadn't bothered to knock.

A hand clapped across my mouth and a piece of paper was stuffed between my clenched fingers.

"Your brother." A man spoke. More wind than voice. He might have been seventeen or forty.

He let me go. The door shut behind him. I didn't dare open it or follow him out.

No, instead I locked it from the inside. I sank to my knees. I wasn't thinking about the heroic things I might have done. I was trying to figure out what had happened! Door opens. Man. Note. Door closes.

In the darkroom's red light, I read "James Moriarty" written on the folded piece of paper.

Why give me a note for James? I tried to understand what was happening.

1) A note could be mailed, so why deliver it in person?

Possibilities:
a) urgency; no time to wait for the mail
b) effect; to scare me, to make sure I passed my fear along to my brother, heightening the importance or significance of the note
c) panic; poor planning on the part of the person who'd written the note, see (a), which

leads naturally to the messenger's feeling threatened or suffering from injury so . . .

2) Why not leave the note in my brother's room; why give it to me?

Possibilities:

a) the messenger doesn't know which room is my brother's room
b) visitors aren't allowed into the dorms—the messenger is not a student or faculty member
c) or . . . the messenger is a student or faculty member but can't risk being seen in a dorm where he doesn't belong
d) the messenger knows me by my face, but not my brother

There had to be others but I couldn't think of them. Coming to my feet, I finally switched on the light.

I ripped the taped edge and unfolded the note.

Ha Clues He

I refolded the note and eased the door open, forgetting all about my photography work. The school's makerspace was empty. I took a step, slipped, and nearly fell. The floor was wet. A small puddle, and from it, wet wheel marks.

A *wombat*? I wondered. A student nickname for the dorm janitors.

Had a wombat passed me the note? It seemed unlikely. A wombat could just slip it under James's door.

For a moment, I considered following the shoe prints. They seemed to aim deeper into the makerspace.

I wasn't feeling brave. Far from it. I was shaking like a leaf.

I took a deep breath and took off running for the Bricks, the school dorms.

Answers could wait.

CHAPTER 7

Wouldn't you know it would have been Lexie Carlisle to read the *Boston Herald*? Who couldn't have guessed that? The small number of students during summer session left the common room pretty empty.

I watched as Lexie stood and walked past the empty couches, benches, and game tables. The plastic ficus trees. Over the semicircular shadows cast by the 1960s-style wood-and-polished chrome chandeliers.

Lexie carried the well-read newspaper tucked under her arm as she searched for James among those awaiting dinner. She shouldn't have had such a hard time finding him, except that James hadn't arrived yet.

Lexie's presence in summer session was likely as bewildering to others as was mine and James's. I expected the reason for Lexie being here for summer session, like ours, was more the result of "what to do with the poor darling?" than anything to do with grades. Her father, like ours, had died. Hers in winter session; ours in fall. James and I had also lost our family driver and all-around-greatest-guy-ever, Ralph, to a nasty car accident. What a year! Lexie's mother wasn't doing well. James and I didn't have a mother. She'd run off for unknown reasons years before. We lived with her absence, never accepting it, but what can you do to change a fact?

The three of us had been swept under a rug for the summer. Lois, our former nanny, who was now employed by our legal guardian to take care of us, simply had no clue what to do with us. Like the two of us, she had been devastated by Ralph's death.

So, there we were, Lexie and I. And it was almost dinnertime. I was spying on her, to be sure, because there was something in the way she carried that newspaper, pinned under her arm like it might as well have been surgically attached. No joke! It wasn't about the sudoku or crossword puzzle. It wasn't about the horoscopes. The newspaper had purpose, something worth clinging to. Maybe what was in it explained how Lexie the Loser had won my brother's attention. For twelve years he and I had been like a person and his shadow. At Baskerville, things were different. At Baskerville, everything had changed.

James entered the room strutting like a crown prince. He had a newfound high opinion of himself and I resented that. The thing was, I knew James to be internally confident but outwardly shy. Somewhere along the line a switch had been thrown. He acted as if he knew something no one else did and that whatever he knew was something everyone wanted to know. Girls noticed him now in ways they hadn't before. Several gestured with small finger-waves in his direction, or offered him a telling smile. It made me sick! The boys fell into two camps: James's camp and those who pretended he didn't exist. But the funny thing was just by pretending, they made James exist all the more. Infuriating.

Lexie saw James. She didn't finger-wave. She didn't smile slyly like the other girls. She turned her back on him, tightening her wing-clasp on the newspaper.

I could be really dense. It was something I could admit to myself, but rarely to another living person. Using this scintillating piece of knowledge, I moved to within range of Lexie and got a good look at her prized newspaper, mentally recording two of the paper's photographs.

I backed away, turned, and found the table where the daily newspapers lay like terrace stairs. Three copies each: *The New York Times*, *Boston Herald*, *Washington Post*, *USA Today*. Untouched, to my surprise. During the school year I would have found only one or two copies, and all wrinkled from over-reading. Summer session really was different!

The photos matched with Lexie's copy. I had the right edition. I sat down and started turning pages quickly, eyes on headlines. In between turns, I monitored both James and Lexie, somehow knowing they were going to find each other. Opposite field magnets, and all of that.

The bottom half of the Metro section's opening page carried four headlines: a drug bust, Boston police security at a hockey game, a major "weather event" predicted the following day. And, top of the page:

PREEMINENT ATTORNEY MURDERED IN MUGGING

My eyes raced across the words, picking and choosing, like running through a field of wild-flowers.

Conrad Lowry, Esq., our family lawyer, had been murdered in Boston. He had hired Lois and Ralph to take care of us after Father's accident. Now his body had been recovered in a park in Roxbury, mentioned as the city neighborhood with the second-highest crime rate. Mr. Lowry dead? I hadn't known him all that well, but he'd worked with Father forever.

Mr. Lowry had been found with no wallet, jewelry, or property on his person. He'd been identified by a dry-cleaning tag pinned onto the lining of his suit jacket. With a shortness of breath, I wondered why Lexie had brought the paper. Did she somehow know this was news James—*and I*—had to know? How could she know Mr. Lowry was our father's attorney?

It was weird the way it affected me. Much too quickly, outrage and fear changed to suspicion. Not so much about Mr. Lowry, although that may have been in my thoughts, but about Ralph's car crash. I don't know why I would have thought about Ralph, but there it was. A car crash. A mugging. My father falling off a ladder. Taken by themselves, the three deaths seemed like bad luck. Wrong place, wrong time kind of thing. The newspaper article made no mention of why Mr. Lowry had been in Roxbury, alone and in a park. Maybe the police were still trying to figure that out. Maybe they'd never know.

James and Lexie found an island of empty space to the left of the massive bay window that looked west, down across tennis courts and the varsity football field to the lush green of endless forest and waves of ever fainter hills. Lexie passed the newspaper to him, her action confirming my earlier concern.

He read; looked up; eyes back to the newspaper; back to Lexie. The two talked and I witnessed confusion on my brother's face. I saw a troubled brow and squinting eyes. He pursed his lips between his spoken words, which from a distance looked like whispering.

But something was missing from his reaction. Something big: *surprise*. Shock. James wasn't the least bit shocked or troubled or grief-stricken by the news. He didn't grab for his phone. Instead, he appeared to carefully read the article. He occasionally consulted Lexie, then read some more. The two looked more like they were discussing a term paper than the death of James's and my legal guardian.

Jealousy filled me like air in a balloon. I was going to burst. That was supposed to be me talking to James, not Lexie. How had she taken over so quickly? Worse: I liked Alexandria Carlisle. She never wore makeup; her uniform's shirt went untucked most of the time, revealing nothing of her figure the way some girls tried so hard to do. She did her own nails, and not often enough. Could look pretty if and when she wanted, which wasn't often. But she'd gone to James about the news. My brother never so much as looked for me in the room. Why hadn't the school told James and me? Was it a surprise to everyone?

I wouldn't know what had been said that night for several weeks.

"We should have helped him," Lexie told James.

"He didn't want us to. I think he knew he was dying. There was no time."

Lexie sniffled.

"I know . . . " James said. "So awful."

Neither spoke for several minutes.

"Who could have moved his body?" Lexie asked James in a whisper. "All the way to Boston? Why? James?"

"Hmm? I suppose someone didn't want him found here."

"But why?" she asked. "Are you listening to me, James?"

"What's that?"

"Why would someone not want—? The headmaster wouldn't order something like that. This can't possibly be about bad publicity!"

"No. I agree. Not the headmaster," James said. "Of course not!"

"You don't sound convinced," Lexie said. James pretended not to hear her. "Who would do such a thing? And why?"

"Really, Lexie? You can't answer that?" He searched her eyes. "Who's the one person who cares about moving a body that's been shot?"

"The person who shot him! The killer!"

"Shh! Not so loud! Yes, the killer."

"*Oh my dog!*" she said. "*Scum of a beach!*"

"Yeah," James said.

"Someone at Baskerville killed your family attorney?" She backed up a step. "James?"

"No! I mean, how should I know?" James groaned. "The riddle. The one he told me not to forget. The Elves and the Shoemaker. Maybe that's a clue. Maybe that's why he wanted me to remember."

"Brothers Grimm. I looked it up," Lexie said. "It's not much of a story. Some naked elves and this old cobbler. The elves make all the shoes for him when he's sleeping at night."

"Naked. Ick," James said. "I looked it up, too."

"Of course you did," Lexie said. "I don't think there's even a moral to it."

"I don't see how it means anything. A shoeshine guy? I don't see a connection."

"It must mean something," she said.

"I think that's overly optimistic," James said.

"Someone shot him, James. Remember hearing that sound?"

James ignored her question. "But what was Lowry doing on school property in the first place? Doesn't make sense." James tried to sound surprised. In fact, he had the explanation: the Scowerers. The secret group met beneath the chapel. But James would have, should have, known of such a meeting.

He had someone he could ask. It would have to wait until after dinner.

The dining room's enormous doors opened, nearly smacking the two. But James pulled Lexie out of the way just in time, and held her arm as they searched for a table.

Mr. Hinchman's dinner table rarely failed to entertain. The boys' varsity soccer coach, and father of two day students (the most beautiful girls on campus), Hinchman had boyish expressions and a willing laugh. He was a favorite of the students. Summer session's light attendance lessened the crush and the rush to find a good seat at his table for dinner. James and Lexie took chairs immediately to Hinchman's right, with Lexie sitting closest to the math teacher.

"Reading the paper, I see," Hinchman said to Lexie. "Wonderful habit to have, Alexandria."

She slipped the paper under her bottom. "I like to keep up with what's going on in Boston."

"Head of the Charles is my favorite event," James said. "The regatta. Ever been?"

"I haven't," said Hinchman. "I hunt on my October Sundays. We have soccer games on Saturdays, of course."

"Hunt? You shoot . . . *animals?*" Lexie said.

"Birds. Ducks. Geese. Yes. And we eat every one."

A disapproving Lexie retreated into string beans and bacon.

"Quail. Pheasant. Diego, named after Diego Maradona, has such a nose. Best hunting dog, ever, bar none."

"I've never seen a hunting dog do his thing," James said. "Is he like a bloodhound?"

"He can scent anything. Absolutely! And birds, he scents naturally. Dogs have a sense of smell forty times that of humans. You're welcome to come out with me sometime this fall, James. Would love to have you."

"I appreciate that."

Lexie leveled James with a look of utter disapproval. But James didn't care. She couldn't see past her green beans. She wasn't thinking. Such moments went to his head, reinforcing his sense of superiority. There were the small-minded people and then there was James Moriarty, purveyor of the entire landscape of possibility.

They got past the meat loaf. Killed the mashed potatoes. Left most of the oily green beans and bacon in the dish. Lexie talked with Hinchman about Diego Maradona's soccer career. James tuned out all conversation, his mind going like a millstone, grinding away the coarse and refining it into something digestible. Let them have their small talk; James had moved on.

"Where did you go?" Lexie asked on their way out of the dining room.

"The point wasn't that he kills birds," James answered. "It's the dog, Lexie."

"I have no idea what you're talking about. Which is nothing new, I might add."

"Ouch!" James said.

They reached outside and a summer evening, warm, no breeze, and the cry of small insects filling their ears. Both of them caught by the perfection of the moment, other students streamed past them as if they were two sticks poking up out of a stream.

Lexie sighed. She reached out tentatively, hooking her pinkie into his. The two remained unmoving, wholly uncomfortable and yet thrilled, not wishing to be anywhere else.

"You're going to explain what you mean," she said softly, "when you're ready."

"Of course."

"I don't like to be left hanging."

"Understood."

"Tuck Shop later?" It was the closest thing to a student lounge. Located in the gymnasium, the Tuck Shop, part food bar, part mini-market, offered a pool table, Ping-Pong, foosball, and a big-screen TV. It opened evenings after study hall and afternoons after athletics.

"Definitely," he said.

She released their fingers and walked away, somehow knowing James needed time to himself.

He congratulated her silently for understanding that, for giving him the time.

He headed away from the other students, in the direction of the school chapel.

CHAPTER 8

SOMEONE HID WITHIN THE BLACKENED SHAD-
ows and the tangled ivy on the far side of the school
chapel.

"Come," James instructed.

A man appeared, dressed in a groundskeeper's
coveralls and heavy work boots; his buzz-cut black
hair revealed a tattoo on his scalp. It being so dark,
James couldn't make out the design.

"Espiranzo! Good to see you."

"And you, Governor."

James wasn't comfortable with his title as head
of the Directory. "The Scowerers?"

"'Tis a busy time, James," said Espiranzo.

"It is. Did you hear the news—a member of the Directory?"

"Slain. Yes."

"Was it us? Did the Scowerers kill him?"

The man cursed boldly. "Mr. Lowry's a member of the Directory. That would never happen. Besides, we are not in the business of ending lives. Least not at present."

"What's that mean?"

"Difficult times, James. You read about the killing, or you heard about it?" Espiranzo asked.

"The article's full of errors."

"Errors hardly matter when one's met his maker."

"He was killed here."

Espiranzo was unmoving. "Where?"

"Here. In the woods. Down the hill."

"Don't be believing every rumor you hear, Governor. 'Twas Boston."

"I saw him. I was with him. He'd been shot."

"Be careful, boy." Espiranzo adopted a paternal, unfavorable tone with James that he did not appreciate.

"Injured badly. Bleeding. I came across him in the woods. I'm not here to get your approval of what I saw with my own eyes. I'm here to ask you, if it wasn't us, if it wasn't the Scowerers, then who would kill him and move his body?"

Espiranzo grabbed James by the arm and pulled him into the darkness with him. A grown-up walked past, following the path to the gap between the stone wall and then across the two-lane road toward the faculty houses beyond.

"How did you know?" James asked in a whisper.

"Heard the man coming."

"Impossible. I was right here. Didn't hear a thing."

"Your senses improve as a matter of course and need," said Espiranzo. "Not to worry, sir. You have much to learn."

They remained in the dark, their backs against the cool, scratchy ivy leaves.

"From here to Boston, and good enough to fool the police," James said.

Espiranzo didn't answer.

"Can't be easy. But more important, what was Lowry up to that someone would kill him or have him killed?"

Still, no answer.

"If you don't know, just say so."

"I don't know," the man said softly. It gave James a shiver.

"I don't want you asking around."

"If what you say is true, it needs explaining."

"One man's dead. That's enough. I didn't like Mr. Lowry, but my father did. Trusted him with so much. With me. With Moria. For all we know, he asked the wrong question. Look, I couldn't bear to lose you too, Espiranzo."

"I don't like the thought much myself."

"The Directory must be told. The Directory only."

"I'll take care of it."

"Immediately." James let the silence that followed speak for him.

"If it's murder, and it happened here as you said— You understand the urgency that creates. Someone's killing our leaders."

"I understand."

"Like it or not, I must stay close to you, sir," said Espiranzo. "'Tis my job. In times such as this, more so than ever."

"You cannot be seen. It would cause too many questions."

"The girl. Is that wise? Do you value her safety?"

James shuddered. The man knew too much. Saw too much. "If there's trouble, you're ordered to protect Lexie first."

"I am not."

"You are now."

"Might be that you and I could do the same work as you and her. Keeping her out of this would be the best protection of all, you don't mind me saying."

"I do . . . mind you saying. She's smart. Very smart. She knows about . . . She was there. Lowry. I need her."

More silence.

"I'm going to the Tuck Shop. Into the woods after that. I suppose I'll feel safer knowing you'll be nearby."

Espiranzo warned, "I'll have another Scowerer with me. Do not mistake him for the enemy."

"Who *are* the enemy, Espiranzo? Who would have shot Lowry?"

"A good deal of thinking must be done, Governor. By you and the Directory. It's not for me. It starts with you and the headmaster and them others. Same as always."

"I'll let Headmaster Crudgeon know that the Directory needs to meet."

"Indeed." Espiranzo exhaled dramatically.

"Now. I have to do this tonight," said James.

In fact, he had other ideas.

CHAPTER 9

O<small>N THE WAY TO MEET</small> L<small>EXIE</small>, J<small>AMES STOPPED</small> beneath a tree to place a phone call. Use of cell phones on campus was prohibited for all students but James and me. Even though the Headmaster allowed us to have them (for our security), it didn't mean we could show off. James kept his eyes open and his voice low.

"Detective Colander?"

"Speaking."

James reintroduced himself to the detective superintendent with Interpol, the global law enforcement agency. He remembered the man as tall, his black hair graying, his teeth stained like a smoker's. Colander's raspy voice confirmed his bad habit. The detective had questioned us at the Interpol offices. He'd put us under surveillance. He'd made a nuisance of himself. But he was a global cop. He knew things and had connections.

"There's a case that should interest you," James continued. "A death."

"Is that so?"

"Lower part of the Metro section. First page. The *Herald*. Today. Hairs and fibers? I don't know what you guys call it. You're going to find leaves and dirt and sticks and stuff like that. If it's a mugging, a shooting, there should be a lot of blood, right? You should check it out."

"Why would I do that, James?"

James hung up the call without saying goodbye. Rude? Yes. But lately James didn't seem to notice the lines between what he wanted and what offended others. Including his sister. He could be a real pain—surprise.

Later, he met up with Lexie in the Tuck Shop. Most nights there was either nut mix, popcorn, Rice Krispie bars, or fruit snacks to take, but it was always gone quickly.

"You promised to explain whatever it was that turned you into a space-out at dinner." Lexie didn't forget much.

"The dog, Lexie. Hinchman's dog is a hunting dog. A scent dog. Do the math."

"Don't be mean."

"Mean? I'm here, aren't I?"

"And don't be so patronizing," Lexie chided.

"Pardon me if I don't want to wait around for others to figure out what I already know! You're boring me, Lexie."

"And you're being a real ashtray."

"Hunting dogs go after the hunter's dead bird, or dead deer, or—"

"Dead body," she whispered, her face suddenly pale. "You can't possibly be thinking what I think you are thinking."

"Of course I'm thinking what you think I'm thinking," James said. "The truth is like a seed stuck in your teeth. Sometimes it just falls out all on its own. Sometimes it hides or it sticks and you have to pick it out. You have to grab a toothpick, dig in there, and pry it loose."

"Diego's your toothpick," Alexandria said.

"Who's Diego?" James said.

"Do you ever pay any attention to anyone other than yourself?"

"Rough."

"Mr. Hinchman's dog, James. *Diego*."

James nodded. "Oh, right. Got it."

"When?"

"Tonight."

"No way."

"Way."

"All black."

"What?" James said.

"We wear all black," Lexie said. "I'll bring red theatrical gel to cover the two flashlights you will provide. Red is much harder to be seen from a distance. What else?"

"Bulletproof vests?"

"Not funny," she said.

"Whistles for if things go bad."

"Badly."

"What?" James asked.

"Never mind."

"The gym," James said. "There are whistles right here in the gym."

"Two, please," she said.

"Got it."

"A camera. Not our phones, but a camera that can shoot in almost no light. In case we find something."

"Of course we're going to find something," James said.

"Natalie has a nice camera. I'll borrow hers."

"Don't tell her anything."

"Yeah, right. 'Hey everybody, I'm going to steal Hinchman's dog with James and go looking for the trail of a dead man who ended up in Boston.'"

"Actually, you could probably get away with saying that. They'd just think you'd lost it."

"We could be expelled, James. Or worse."

"Two a.m.," he said. "Back by four."

"And if whoever did this is still out there?" she asked.

"Then I suppose we're not back by four." They met eyes. Neither blinked for a long time, and when it happened, it was James first.

"That . . . is . . . not . . . funny," Lexie said, fighting back her grin.

James looked smugly proud of himself.

Summer air after midnight held different qualities than daytime air. Summer scents held flowers, cut grass, and loamy earth. Even the hint of barbecue somewhere within it all. Like charcoal and chlorine. Low tide and high mountain pine.

At night, crickets chirped. Frogs croaked. Leaves rustled. And then, there were moments of absolute stillness that could be terrifying.

Lexie was not one to allow herself to be led, so

she and James walked side by side. Dressed as ninjas. James with a red-occluded headlamp, courtesy of Lexie's red theatrical gel. Lexie feeling self-conscious about her tight-fitting top and wishing she'd gone with the T-shirt. James feeling stupid for having spread the football team's eye black onto his cheeks as camo. Both feeling awkward while trying to project confidence.

They'd agreed on a few primitive hand signals to avoid speaking. The gag rule was supposed to last until they got Diego back in his cage. An hour or two of silence. Neither believed it would hold.

James brought beef jerky to attract Hinchman's dog to the cage door. It worked. The only sound the dog made was the pounding of his tail against the wire mesh cage. James got the gate open and the dog out as Lexie watched the house for a light coming on, or movement in any of its windows.

They avoided the road down to the hockey rink just in case, staying inside a strip of woods that dropped from behind faculty housing to the varsity football field and joined the hundred acres or more of rolling forest. They walked carefully, eyes on the ground, trying to avoid snapping sticks or tearing through brambles. Diego heeled to James without being instructed.

Once well into the forest, James opened his

backpack and removed Lowry's lone shoe, inserting the dog's snout a good way inside. The dog huffed and grew excited. James, who'd internet-searched hunting dog commands, lifted the dog's flapping ear and whispered, "Find it!" The only words spoken over the past thirty minutes.

Diego was all business, putting his nose to the ground and dragging James along by the leash. James and Lexie followed the dog lower on the hill, reaching the top border of the capture-the-flag boundary. Minutes later they passed through no-man's-land, each consumed by different memories of the same night.

Lexie reached over and took James's hand. He didn't try to let go. He didn't look over at her either. They continued as a connected trio—James with the leash, Lexie with James.

James switched on his red headlamp and waved his hand, signaling: *unsure.*

Lexie pointed to the right and then made the same *unsure* motion. James tugged the leash. The dog led them in that direction. Their progress continued a few yards at a time, both Lexie and James looking for anything that might jar their recollection of how they'd come across the opening where Lowry had appeared.

After another twenty minutes of slow going,

Lexie steered them back uphill. James didn't protest. They came into the clearing from a different spot, but there was no mistaking it, in no small part because Diego was pulling so hard he was about to break the leash. They reached the ruffled leaves that were black in places and looking as if ink had been spilled. But it wasn't ink.

James used the shoe again. Lexie cupped some of the leaves and held the dried blood to the dog. Diego practically pulled out of his own fur.

Showtime! It was as if the dog were following a cable hidden beneath the leaves. He tacked this way and that, but never far off a center line that carefully dodged bushes and shrubs—just as Lowry had. At the occasional tree trunk the dog went berserk, sniffing and huffing, snorting and coughing. It became clear to both Lexie and James that Lowry had paused at these locations, not only because of Diego, but also the discovery of similarly black-splattered leaves at the tree's base. And, in one instance, a perfect impression of a human handprint on the bark of a birch tree.

It was the handprint that caused Lexie to vomit. Kneeling off by herself, she retched and puked and dry-heaved as tears flowed from her eyes. Too soon to the death of her father, James supposed. Too real when intertwined with the idea of a hunting dog and men having pursued Lowry in much the same way. James dragged Diego over to Lexie and she came into his arms and they hugged. And the dog wrapped the leash around them. And their chests moved as if laughing. James kissed a tear from her cheek. She leaned back and glared at him. Maybe she hadn't liked it. Maybe she didn't know how to react. James felt much older.

"Thank you," Lexie said.

"No problem."

"Don't do that again. Don't confuse things."

"Understood," James said.

"I mean . . . not unless you ask me."

"OK."

"But you *can* ask me."

"OK," James said.

"Are you mad? You look mad. I didn't mean to make you mad. It . . . I liked it. I appreciate it, James."

"I'm not mad." *Confused*, James wanted to say. Girls were confusing.

Moving once again, the dog followed Lowry's climb up the hill. James signaled a stop. He and Lexie caught their breath as James ad-libbed swinging a stick—a hockey stick—and pointed north to indicate the rink.

Diego's frantic behavior infected them both.

The dog reared up on his hind legs, straining the leash. He wanted to get on with the hunt.

James took Lexie's hand this time. He gave it a slight squeeze. The pace was hurried, the climb difficult. James pulled them to stop, resisting Diego's uphill charge. He cupped his ear, imploring Lexie to listen along with him. Wings—probably bats; Lexie didn't want to look up. Insects sang loudly. And what was *that*? Lexie wondered. A door? A window? A car? She pointed behind. She wanted to turn around and head back.

James shook his head. He motioned they should hunch over and continue more carefully, his fingers making like walking legs. She nodded, though reluctantly. Taking James by the shoulder, she pointed to herself and then away, suggesting they split up. James shook his head. Retook her hand.

All for one and one for all, he seemed to be saying. She shrugged. Waited. Nodded. Joined him and the dog, her legs heavier, her feet less willing.

James sensed progress, complimented himself on using Diego. Slipped the dog some more jerky. They weren't following a rabbit or a deer. They were following Lowry's death march back to the source. Back to where he'd been shot?

The first time I heard anything about any of this was when I was awakened by a text.

A text from James.

> If I'm not at school tomorrow, start looking for me here

Attached was an internet-mapped pin with a GPS coordinate.

It took me a second to zoom the map so I could see the pin's location. I searched for a landmark I knew.

I gasped so loud I woke up my roommate, Natalie.

My brother was out of his mind. I had to stop him.

CHAPTER 10

Down through the dark forest James and Lexie moved, surrounded now by the whining of insect wings, the high-pitched croaking of tree frogs, the unexplained creaking of tree limbs. Like doors on rusted hinges.

James carried the lone shoe with him as he and Lexie followed the snorting dog.

Diego kept the leash tight and the pace faster than James would have wanted. The dog was strong and determined.

Long minutes passed, feeling longer. Muscles strained and grew sore. Lexie did not complain, did not speak. But eventually she ran her hand down James's outstretched hand, running shivers up his spine as she took the leash from him, slipping her hand through the loop with his. James withdrew his hand without complaint—his shoulder feeling as if it were out of joint. He wished he could have kept it in the leash with hers just a few seconds more. He fell behind, placing his hand on her left shoulder to keep them together in lockstep. Her shoulder was warm to the touch.

Diego picked up a strong scent. Nose to the ground. The hair on his back raised like a porcupine. He was a heat-seeking missile now. He was locked in as he turned them back up the hill slightly and then traversed. Lexie held the leash with both hands. Lacking the proper commands, they had no way of stopping him even if they wanted to.

"He's heading back to where I found Lowry," James said over her shoulder. "We need to turn him around. We need to know where Lowry *got shot*."

Together they shortened the leash and, with all their strength, reversed the dog, aiming him.

Maneuvering past boulders and trees, James and Lexie nearly screamed when a squirrel leaped in the branches overhead.

They came to a stream. Diego hesitated, then returned to random patterns. He snorted and sniffed. James led him downstream.

"Did you hear that?" Lexie whispered.

"No. I'm pretty focused on Diego. What?"

"Never mind."

"Lots of noises in the woods at night."

"If you're trying to reassure me, it isn't working," Lexie said. "Footsteps, I think. A voice, that is, a grunt, like someone bumping into something."

Diego pulled. They jumped over the stream. James realized how the noise of the dog barreling along let only the louder unexpected sounds through. What if Lexie had heard someone? he wondered. He walked close to her, speaking more softly than the sounds from the dog.

"I think Lowry may have tried to use the stream to cover his tracks," James said.

"You sound like your roommate," Lexie said quietly.

"Former roommate. Not anymore. Good riddance. Him being expelled from school was the best thing that ever happened to this place."

"To the school, or to you?"

"Have you been talking to Moria or something?"

"Or something," Lexie said.

"Meaning?" he asked.

"You and Sherlock were a good influence on each other."

"Since you knew him so well," James said sarcastically.

"You're different now that he's gone."

"Different good, or different bad?"

"Just different."

"More . . . what?"

"He's a smart boy. It never hurts to be around smart people. They tend to make you smarter."

"But you're a loner."

"Exactly. I hang around with a smart girl."

"Yourself? Haha! Wait, are you saying I'm not as smart with Sherlost gone?"

"You said it. I didn't."

"Ouch!" James said. "That really hurts, Lexie."

"Good. It should. No pain, no gain, right? You hang around with losers, James. Troublemakers. Centigrade IQs. You should be on the Fahrenheit scale. The Holmes kid . . . I had him in a couple classes. The proctors were afraid of him. He has that kind of smarts, that effect on people. That effect on you."

James said nothing for several minutes. Diego led them to the valley floor and then started up the opposing hill.

"You're mad at me," Lexie said.

"No. I love being called stupid."

"If that's what you got out of that, then yes, you are." She left James a few yards behind her.

"OK. I know what you're saying about guys like Thorndyke. I get it. But there's stuff going on. More than I can . . . I can't really talk about it. But there's more."

"And there you are, sounding so brilliant."

"Oh, come on!"

"You're better than that, James. You're better than thugs and secrets and thinking you live in a world the rest of us don't. It's snobbish. It's rude. It isn't you."

"What if it is?" James asked.

"Then . . . then you're the one on your own, not me."

"You're breaking up with me?"

"Breaking up? We're not dating! Eww! What are you talking about?"

"I mean, breaking off our friendship."

"Friendships don't get broken, they get abandoned. And no, I'm not abandoning you. But it doesn't mean I won't."

James stewed. The hill proved a difficult climb, and Lexie was in far better shape than him. As she and the dog pulled away from James, he too thought he heard someone out there. The woods played tricks with sound. It deflected off tree trunks and ricocheted off rocks. It rose into the canopy of branches overhead and came back down like a drizzle. There was no placing it.

But there was no denying it either.

Lexie was right: they weren't alone.

CHAPTER 11

IT APPEARED FROM THE DARK WOODS AS A CRUM-
bling stone fort or castle. Given the lack of light, it
looked two-dimensional, like a painted backdrop
to a stage play. Braided vines and ivy clung to the
structure's remains: graffiti-covered rock walls,
missing windows in some places.

"Looks like Narnia or something," Lexie
gushed, holding Diego back from the set of rising
steps.

"That part, up the stairs. That's an observatory. The school's, I suppose. I knew we had one.
Never knew where it actually was."

"Like with a telescope?" Lexie asked.

"Exactly."

"It's huge."

"Apparently."

"Lowry was in there before he was in the woods." Lexie didn't make it a question.

"Diego certainly seems convinced." The dog pulled so hard he rose to just his hind legs and then coughed and came back down to all fours.

"Stargazing got him killed? That seems unlikely."

"Highly unlikely," agreed James. "Though I can see a meeting taking place out here. A place like this. A secret meeting."

"Why would your family lawyer, from Boston, take a secret meeting in the school observatory?"

Shaped like a silo, the structure had a domed roof with a retractable metal section. It was just weird enough to look dangerous.

Lexie lowered her voice. "What if he was shot in there? What are we doing here, James? So now we know he was in there. We should get out of here. We have to get Diego back soon anyway. You should call that detective."

"We should see if it's open," James said.

"Are you *nuts*?"

"We have Diego. Maybe he can help inside."

"How? We're here. That's nuts."

"I want to go in there," James said.

"No way."

"Think about it. We're right here. Lowry was inside the observatory."

"I am thinking about it. I'm thinking about how fast I can run. How fast I can get back to school and into bed. Go inside? Are you kidding me?" Lexie passed James the leash. "Have fun."

Lexie took a couple steps downhill. The sound of sticks breaking in the woods stopped her short. "James . . ." she hissed.

"I know," James said equally softly. "I heard it too. Please, don't go. Not on your own."

"Says the big, tough boy."

"I didn't mean it like that."

"You're coming with me. And you're coming *right now*." She looked up at the curving dome of the observatory. "I don't like it here."

"Hold on to this." James tried to pass her the leash. She wouldn't take it. He tried again, prying her crossed arms apart, and wrapped the leash around her wrist. "Stay."

"Oh, very funny."

James raced up the steps.

"No!" she said harshly. "Do not—"

James leaned on the lever door handle. His

shoulders slumped. "Locked."

"There is a God," Lexie said.

He tried it again. Funny, it was still locked. He bounded down the stairs and vaulted the handrail.

"Show-off," she said.

"We'll get the key. We'll return the dog. Get back to the dorm before we're caught. We can come here again in the daylight."

"Maybe *you* can. I've seen enough."

"Don't you want to know what happened?" he asked.

"Not if it means the same thing happens to me."

"You really think the killer stuck around? Why would anyone do that?" he said.

Another crack of twigs, this time coming closer. Lexie stood up taller than she was. Her jaw trembled. "I hope we're not about to find out."

CHAPTER 12

BEING THE BRIGHTER OF THE TWO MORIARTY children, and the only girl, I went about trying to figure out the note that had been forced upon me.

Ha Clues He

First I broke it down. "Ha" had to mean something funny. "Clues," I knew exactly what a clue was. "He," I thought it probably meant James.

funny clues James

It didn't make sense. How could a clue be funny? And why would I care about a funny clue even if I could figure out what a funny clue was?

James clues funny

James funny clues

A clue to make James laugh? A clue *about* James that would make me laugh? It seemed unimportant. Why all the drama to deliver me a stupid note?

The answer to all my questions was simple: *What would Sherlock do?*

The weird, skinny little creature was an expert when it came to figuring things out. I could no longer text him because he'd been sent home to England. But he did answer emails. So, I wrote him. Despite the time difference, he replied almost immediately.

My dear M:

It looks like a word scramble to me. Have you tried an anagram generator?

Yours,
SH

Leave it to Lock. I did as he said. The online anagram generator rearranged the letters of the three words into a list of every possible combination.

Of the many results, only a few came back with actual words instead of gibberish. These were:

Leaches Uh

A Such Heel

Ha Such Eel

Ah Clue She

Ash Clue He

I took them one by one.

Leaches Uh

Could I accept a misspelling? A homonym? In olden days leeches had been used to cure bruising. Was I being warned that someone else, maybe even me, was going to be beat up?

A Such Heel

A "heel" was a pest. "Such a Heel" could mean "what a pest." Was I annoying someone? Maybe that was a good thing?

Ha Such Eel

This one intrigued me because Sherlock, Ralph, and I had once infiltrated a fishery in Boston—an adventure that had nearly gotten us hurt. Since then, Ralph had been killed in a car accident, an event that James had yet to recover from. Was this a clue to return to the fishery?

Ah Clue She

A clue for me? Something that would make me think "Aha!"? What could it be? What was I missing?

Ash Clue He

Now we were getting somewhere! Father had hidden a secret key to his desk in the ashes of his office fireplace. That key had opened a secret room with treasures galore. Also, a notebook and other items that were of serious interest to James and me. Note to self: I had never checked *the rest of the ashes* to see if anything else was hidden. How stupid of me! Maybe I could let Lois in on the secret and ask her to search for me and report back.

CHAPTER 13

THE QUESTION JAMES HAD TO ASK HIMSELF WAS this: What did Sherlock Holmes do with his (illegal) copy of the master key to the school? James's annoying roommate had been expelled from Baskerville Academy at the end of the school year, forced to return to England. Sherlock Holmes was too logical to take such a prized possession with him. He wouldn't have hidden it, James thought. He wouldn't have tossed it. He would have . . .

. . . *given it to his best friend.*

That was me, of course. Being my brother, James also knew that he was the last person on earth with whom I would share it—or anything, for that matter. I'd have rather turned it over to Headmaster Crudgeon.

So, James began to plot, a skill he'd developed over the past twelve months. Perfected, might be closer to the truth. James sneaked into my room on a Tuesday night when he knew I was in the photo lab and my roommate, Natalie, was off watching a movie with a friend. A boy in the girls' dorm was strictly against the rules and cause for suspension or expulsion. This accounted for two of his goons standing watch, prepared to whistle a warning if they saw a proctor anywhere nearby.

My brother searching my room was nothing new. It had been a regular event in our shared childhood. I'd often stolen his diary or "borrowed" a particular toy.

He knew my hiding places as well as I knew his. He didn't bother with my closet shelves—too obvious. Instead, he searched the pockets of my hanging clothes. I'd been hiding stuff there for years now. Whoever pats down a dress or jacket in a closet? The toes of my shoes—I would stuff the ends with tissue so nothing fell out; you had to go looking for the hidden prize. My pillowcase was another spot. My duvet unzipped at the bottom: a good place to hide papers. Hiding his journal or my own diary took more effort. For that I used an old textbook. They worked the best because the books were bigger, and fatter, than normal books. I cut and removed the insides of pages with a razor blade, creating a framed hole in which I could hide another, smaller book. The nice thing about this: no one bothered to look inside a fourth-grade math book. Even if/when James searched my library— which I'm pretty sure he'd done before—he would have gone right past any textbook, and thereby missed what he was searching for.

Ten minutes spent nervously ransacking my side of the dorm room, and James had nothing to show for his efforts. No master key. He checked my costume jewelry box, and it was during this process a thought occurred.

"I found this photo of us at Christmas," James told Lexie. The two of them walking together after lunch, back toward Main House, drew a number of eyeballs and spawned some instant rumors. Schools thrived on such rumor, and summer school wasn't any different except there were fewer of us, and therefore fewer stories to exaggerate into rumor. Though the students still gave it their best effort.

"You and Moria," Lexie said. She noticed people staring much more than did James. In my opinion, boys are pretty much oblivious creatures.

"Right. We went down to the Cape house with Ralph and Lois. It was pretty awkward with Dad not being there. Lois cried a lot. Moria walked the beach, looking out as if maybe Dad was going to show up in a boat or something. Pitiful."

"It's sweet. Don't say that!"

"But there's a photo Ralph took." James's voice trailed off. Maybe he didn't even realize he stopped speaking. He and Ralph had grown super close. Ralph's dying so soon after Father had knocked James sideways. Looking back on it now, I can understand what happened to James. I suppose it makes sense in some way. If there's nothing good left to hold on to, at least hold on to something. James had reached out and taken hold of the Scowerers. Or maybe they'd taken hold of him. He'd have been better off just giving things time—that's what I had to do. Maybe I reached out for Sherlock. But the school took him away from me, and I didn't go all Darth Vader the way James eventually did. My and my brother's choices were totally different. He turned left where I went right. If we were both Alice in Wonderland, I was trying to climb out of the hole back to sunlight; James was only digging deeper.

"The photo," Lexie said, filling the silence James had left. "Tell me about the photo."

"Right! So, in the photo, Moria isn't wearing a necklace."

"And that's important because . . . ?"

"She wears one now."

"James, we're girls. We accessorize."

"It's one of those rawhide strings, like a leather shoelace for a boot. Your idea of accessorizing?"

"It's not my neck. Not my decision."

"You know what I think? I think she started wearing that about the time Sherlost got thrown out. I think she's wearing the key around her neck, not so much as a key but because it belonged to Sherlost. And don't say that's sweet."

"But it is!"

"Please! It's so *Message in a Bottle*! Ewww."

"And you're telling me this because . . . ?" In a very short time, Lexie had learned to read James in ways James didn't want to be read. "You want me to do what, exactly? Reach down her top and pull out the necklace? Not happening, FYI."

"What if she takes it off when she's showering?"

"What are you saying, James?"

"It's leather. Leather stuff gets ruined by water. I'll bet she takes it off."

"And I sneak into her dorm bathroom and steal it?"

"Well . . ."

"I'm not Thorndyke or Eisenower! I'm not stealing for you!"

"It's not like I can get inside a girls' bathroom."

"I should hope not! By the way, you wouldn't like it. Girls are slobs. Worse than boys, I promise you."

"So?"

"This is your problem, not mine. Don't try to put this on me."

"We need the key to get inside the observatory."

"Which is stupid. You heard that person in the woods."

"A deer. Raccoon."

"You don't believe that any more than I do. Someone was following us. Followed us there. Followed us back. It was terrifying."

"Exciting."

"Terrifying. You do not want to go into that observatory."

"So that's why you're not going to help me?"

"Nice try. That stuff won't work on me, James. I'm helping you by not stealing from a friend."

"Randolph's pool party."

"What about it?"

"Friday night."

"I *know* that, James!"

"If she takes it off there in order to swim, I could . . . it could easily just disappear."

"And if she doesn't . . . take it off?" Lexie said.

James's eyes lit up. He stopped her on the path, took her face in his hands, and kissed her before he'd even thought of what he was doing. It was just a reaction. And, judging by Lexie's expression, one he regretted immediately.

"Hey!"

"Sorry!"

"What the . . . ? People saw that! People just *saw you kiss me*! Are you out of your mind? Lexie the Loser? Remember me?"

"Don't say that!"

"You had no right!"

"I know!" He said this three times, very fast. "I'm sorry!"

Lexie leaned back. "You are?"

"What? Yeah . . . I mean, no. I mean, I'm sorry I embarrassed you, but I'm not sorry that I kissed you. But I am sorry that I kissed you without asking you."

She leaned forward and pecked another kiss

onto his lips. "There!" she said. "Maybe that will shut you up."

It did, in fact. "But I thought . . ."

"Less thinking, James. Much less thinking. Good night." She headed for her dorm, leaving James to wonder what exactly had just happened.

Only then did he remember his diabolical idea of how to get the key from around my neck. Only then did he smile.

CHAPTER 14

MR. RANDOLPH'S POOL-AND-DANCE PARTY WAS one of those horrible ideas thought up by grown-ups. It might as well have been called the Awkward Moment Fest. Throw forty kids together, half of whom are embarrassed about bizarre changes to their bodies, ask them to take most of their clothes off, and then get the remaining clothes wet just to make sure they stick to all the embarrassing places. Then, turn on music and have them attempt to dance or, in the case of most of us, jump up and down and call it dancing.

Throw in ribs and coleslaw and soda, just to

make sure the kids are gassy, potato and corn chips to make sure everyone will break out in zits in the coming days, and you have all the ingredients for a terrific time.

At least I wore a one-piece. Some of the girls who showed up in bikinis had earned it. Others, not so much. They made fools of themselves. My one-piece was dark purple. Given my overall shape-lessness, I looked something like a ripe eggplant. But I owned it. If I was going to be an eggplant, I was going to be one with square shoulders, a high chin, and confidence. Lois had taught me that being a woman started with attitude. Let the rest fall where it may.

So I was the dudette with attitude.

Turns out, eggplants can make a pretty big splash when connecting with water. They can also float, dive, and are capable of laughing, though not at the same time. An eggplant with her hair back looks pretty much like the fruit. With her hair down, she looks like a girl *wearing* an eggplant below her shoulders and above her legs. This was my decision: hair down.

I didn't want to attend Mr. Randolph's pool party for all the obvious reasons. But when I heard the list of who wasn't going, I knew I had to attend, or I'd be associated with them and that would condemn me to a life of convents and caring for the homeless. Or ringing bells at Christmastime outside the supermarket. Or the group of kids that ride to eighth-grade graduation—I mean: what?—in a stretch limousine. I was going. And I was not going to be an eggplant on a chaise lounge lawn chair, that is, an eggplant on display, like all that produce at the market under the automatic spritzers. A partially submerged eggplant was difficult to see, so I spent approximately 99 percent of my time partially submerged.

This included Marco Polo, swim contests, underwater swim contests, diving for hoops, and using kickboards. It also included toes and fingers the texture of prunes. There was a good deal of squealing—not my favorite. Boys pushing other boys into us girls—pointless. Swimming between the other person's legs—awkward. And girls tugging constantly on their suits to prevent wedgies.

It was during a game of piggyback Sir Lancelot, when I rode the shoulders of Carol Johansen, from Minneapolis, of Norwegian heritage, a girl who in ninth grade stood just shy of six feet tall, that I found myself facing my brother, James. He rode Bret Thorndyke. Bret was to the student body what those Budweiser horses are to equines. Even with me mounted on Carol's abnormally broad shoulders, our duo looked tiny next to Thorndyke and James.

They came at us at a charge. Carol squealed (see earlier note); I recoiled. Feeling me falling off, Carol used her strength to rock me forward and into my brother. We wrestled for somewhere right around a tenth of a second. That would prove to be a world record against the Thorndyke/Moriarty team, but at the time it meant I was propelled forward by Carol and then to the side by James.

That was when a swimming eggplant became a flying eggplant. And then, the flying eggplant became a drowning eggplant, because the eggplant was laughing so hard when she hit the water.

When I surfaced, coughing, laughing, and splashing, I didn't see James. For a moment, I felt giddy: Could I have possibly pulled James off with me? Had we fought to a draw?

No such luck. He bobbed to the surface a few seconds after me and stretched out his hand. "Sorry! I yanked this off!" he said.

I'd never felt it go.

In his hand was my Sherlock necklace and the prized master key to the school. It would have been a disaster to lose it. I threw my arms around James to thank him as he struggled to continue treading water.

"You're the best brother ever!" I said, while hugging him.

At the time, I couldn't make out why, after such a heroic deed, he looked back at me with such an odd and unusual expression. It looked as if he might cry.

CHAPTER 15

"I LIKE DAYTIME BETTER," LEXIE TOLD JAMES as they climbed the hill toward the observatory. Their side of the hill was already in shadow, as the sun was edging toward dusk after a hot and humid day. "But I don't love the fact that we're not hearing what we heard the other night."

"That's ridiculous."

"Because that means something was out there the other night. It wasn't just forest noises or we'd be hearing them now."

James had to think that through. "Oh. I suppose

that's possible, but it's also because it was night and it isn't now."

"Whatever. I like it better." They continued up the hill. "And remember, I'm not coming in there with you. No way."

James grunted. In fact, he was surprised she'd come along with him, but wasn't about to say so. They would have to time it just right to make it back for dinner. Missing dinner was a risk, a gamble worth taking to avoid returning in the dead of night.

They arrived at the observatory, its domed tower reaching up into the pink-tinted sky.

"We don't even know the key will work," James said. "But that starwatching club meets here on weekends, so it must." He turned the key. He was inside.

Lexie stood guard. "So?" she called in.

"Shh! Not so loud." His footsteps reverberated softly as he crossed the interior. "There's dried blood on the floor."

"Ewww."

"It's *evidence*. He was here. He was definitely here!" James sounded like he'd won the lotto. "Hang on."

Lexie couldn't take it any longer. She craned her head around.

The telescope was wider and shorter than she'd expected. It connected to gears and motors, but was otherwise a disappointment. Along the wall was what appeared to be a control area with a computer and a bank of switches. Other than that, the place was empty. Just a big round empty tower.

She couldn't see any blood from where she stood. James was across the room at a door. He tried his key. It didn't fit. He tried again, which seemed stupid to her, but she didn't say anything. He crossed back to her.

"The drops lead to that door, but it's a different key," James said.

Lexie tried to process the information.

"He was shot on the other side of that door somewhere."

"You're saying he was shot in a storage closet inside the school observatory." Lexie sounded extremely skeptical. Sarcastic.

"I'm not saying it makes sense."

"Because it doesn't," she said.

"Don't you dare say something about how you wish Sherlock was here."

"You have a real thing about him, don't you?"

James didn't answer.

"For your information, that wasn't anywhere on my mind," she said. "But clearly, it was on yours."

"Colander," James said. "Cops want evidence. This is evidence."

"Evidence that you and I broke school rules. Evidence that you must have a master key, or how'd you get in here? Evidence that's going to get you and me thrown out. You'd better think about that, James."

"They can compare these drops to Mr. Lowry's. They'll match. That's all they need."

"Are you listening? They're going to ask questions, James. Questions you can't answer."

James squinted, deep in thought. "So, I'll find all this by accident," he said. He waved his hand to indicate the stains on the floor.

"By accident," Lexie said, disbelieving.

"It's the weekend. What happens every weekend?"

"A movie in Hard Auditorium."

"The Starcatcher Club meets at ten o'clock. Right here. Mr. Royce."

"You're going to join the Starcatcher Club." She wasn't asking.

"No, Lexie. *We* are."

CHAPTER 16

JAMES MISSED BREAKFAST. I NOTICED, AND I WAS pretty sure Lexie did as well.

James had gone into town. The school shopping bus did a quick round trip to the supermarket and drugstore twice a week. The morning trips were hurried, so the kids scattered down rows looking for everything from cereal to toothpaste. But James found his way to the supermarket's coffee bar, where a girl with blue hair and a lip piercing was humming to herself while wiping the counter by the biscotti. James ordered an English Breakfast tea with steamed milk and a piece of banana bread.

He paid up and turned to take a seat, nearly spilling his drink in the process.

Superintendent Colander looked at him from a nearby table. Even though James had agreed to meet him here, seeing the man startled him. The man's graying hair and ice blue eyes reminded James of a husky. He looked tall even sitting down.

"Agent . . . Detective . . . I didn't see you come in."

"Sit," Colander said. He directed James into a chair. "If you're seen talking to an adult, we could both get in trouble." This apparently explained Colander taking a seat at a different table, his back to James. "You said it was urgent. I got up early for this."

"You were going to bring me something," James said.

"The blank key? Yes. You'll find it in your left pocket."

"No way," James said, reaching into his pants pocket. "Oh my gosh! How did you do that?"

"Tricks of the trade. I could show you—"

"But you'd have to kill me. Very funny. That is *such* an old joke."

"You obviously know how to use it, or you wouldn't have asked for it."

"Wiggle it around so the parts of the lock

scratch the metal. Seems pretty easy."

"Cutting it won't be."

"We have a metal shop at school."

"Of course you do. So tell me," Colander said. "What's this evidence you've found?"

Espiranzo had reported back that he'd failed to turn up any Scowerers with knowledge of Lowry's killing. He also hadn't bawled out James for sneaking off into the woods, which meant James had managed to avoid him. James wasn't sure how much to share with the superintendent. What would get him into trouble, and what would be OK?

"Blood. Mr. Lowry's blood. I'm positive. We—I—kind of borrowed a hunting dog. The dog led me to the place."

"At school?"

"Near. It's the observatory. It's across the valley from the campus. In this old ruin. Lowry was inside the observatory. The blood being there is proof."

"That's very good, James."

"I thought you'd like it."

"Explaining any of this won't be easy. His body was found in Boston, don't forget."

"I haven't forgotten."

"As a witness, you're young. You may not be taken seriously at first." Colander sounded concerned.

"It's evidence."

"I understand that."

"So what are you saying?" James asked.

"I don't think it wise for you to suddenly show up as a witness. Whoever killed Mr. Lowry might not appreciate there being a witness."

"That's reassuring."

"I need to think this through, to create a way for me or the local sheriff to pick up on some of this without involving you."

"What about I call nine-one-one? A student. They don't know what student."

"They'd record your voice."

"So I change it. Right?"

"Could work, but I still need to think about it first. A local investigation wouldn't find its way to me."

"What about I call the *Putnam Recorder*? Let some reporter investigate it?"

"You have a good mind, James."

"Is that a yes?"

"That's a maybe."

"I thought guys like you, agents, detectives, act on evidence."

"We do on TV. In real life we need to consult lawyers and make sure we build a legal case. Evidence means nothing if it doesn't hold up in court."

"I'm confused. Are you going to help me or not?"

James never heard a chair move, never had any indication Colander had ditched him. But when he turned around, the man was no longer there.

CHAPTER 17

THE STARCATCHER CLUB WELCOMED ITS TWO new visitors and shared the walk down the long hill, past the ice rink, and up the other side to the crumbling estate and its refurbished observatory. Mr. Royce prattled on about the history of the club and other nonsense for which James had little patience.

Lexie's assignment was to distract the group long enough for James to attempt to mark the blank key by forcibly rocking it in the closet's locked door. She would need to not only win their attention, but make enough noise to cover for him.

They had everything so carefully planned out. Then, Mr. Royce turned on the observatory's bright lights.

The bloodstains were gone.

CHAPTER 18

"I THOUGHT I MIGHT FIND YOU HERE," LEXIE
said. She had done a decent job of distracting
members of the Starcatcher Club an hour earlier by
pretending to roll her ankle.

James had put a blank key into the closet
door and had wiggled it enough to scratch it up.
The things a boy could learn on the internet! she
thought.

She had refused to join him until and unless he
explained his plan, a plan that now involved cutting the key in the school's metalsmith workshop,
part of the makerspace.

James was using a band saw to notch the blank key.

Lexie continued speaking, shouting above the roar. James wore goggles and a noise-suppression headset that reminded her of the kind worn by airport workers. "Curfew's in fifteen minutes."

James maintained his focus.

"If you're so determined to open that door, why don't you just pry it open or something?"

"Because then someone would know I'd opened it."

"So what?"

"As in: Lowry's killer. Or killers. That's what."

"So how stupid are you?" She waited. He didn't say anything. "We'll get in trouble for doing this," she reminded him.

"Go on then. Go back to the dorm!"

So, he was hearing her, she realized. "It was probably just a janitor," she said, referring to the observatory's clean floor.

"Do you believe that?" he asked.

"Why not?"

"Believe what you want."

"You think it was cleaned on purpose?"

"I happened to look at the floor. The mop left a narrow line of water marks between the closet and the main door. Nowhere else. What do you think?"

"You're not going back there without me."

"I wasn't aware I had to get your permission." He never took his eyes off the key.

"Now you do."

"I don't think so."

"Think again."

He stopped working. Shut off the band saw. Lifted the goggles and slipped back the headset so that his right ear stuck out like a bird wing. "I'm going tonight, Lexie. After curfew. You don't like it at night, therefore I'm going by myself. I'm a big boy. I'll be fine."

"You're thirteen!"

"Fourteen. Fifteen, next month."

"Same difference," she said.

"Not really."

"You need a lookout."

"I could use a lookout," James said. "No doubt. But all I *need* is this key, and my phone to take pictures of whatever's in that closet."

"What if it's a mess in there?"

"Probably cleaned that up as well. Colander waited too long. I knew something like this would happen." James sounded so sure of himself.

"We should leave it alone. You know that, right?"

"I thought you didn't want me going alone?" James seemed to be teasing her.

"I'm just saying."

"The question is: *What* are you saying?"

"A man was killed, James. Shot. He's dead, by the way. Let's say you're right and someone cleaned up the floor on purpose. That person is not going to be real thrilled about us poking around. You know?"

"I'm poking. You're the lookout."

"I can't talk to you if you're not going to take this seriously." Lexie crossed her arms.

"You want to talk about serious? They killed my father. Maybe they killed *your* father, too. Oh, yes, Lexie, and I know that's why you're helping me."

"Is not!" Her crossed arms suddenly gripped so tightly she sounded choked.

"Now Lowry."

Lexie was breathing deeply, arms crossed defiantly, ready to slap James. Slap him hard, right across the face.

"It's okay to want answers," James said. "And I can see you're about to cry, and that's okay, too. Even if you are a sissy."

Lexie sprayed a laugh. Her nose ran. She hid her face from him.

James held the key away from them both—it was still very hot from the cutting—and hugged her with one arm. He thought it was such an awkward thing to do, was surprised it didn't feel that way.

She kept her face buried in her hands and sobbed, her hair tickling his chin. She must have stayed that way for five minutes. Felt more like twenty.

"Sorry," she said.

"You got snot on my shirt."

She laughed and dragged her sleeve across her face. She looked a mess. "Why would the same people . . . ?" She couldn't finish the sentence.

"Yeah. I have no idea. That was harsh. I shouldn't have said it. Sorry."

"No . . . you're probably right. Definitely right about me. It *is* why I want to help. I need to understand why . . . it happened."

"You mean it's not true love?"

She laughed again. "'Fraid not."

"I'm heartbroken." Sometimes there was a good deal of truth in a joke, James realized.

"I'm sure you are."

He didn't know what to say. To tell her that he liked her more than as just a friend, or to listen to what she was telling him and keep his trap shut? He stuttered trying to speak. Something told him he was both way too nervous and about to say the wrong thing.

"So, are you in or not?" he asked.

"Tonight?"

"Back of the gym. Two a.m.?"

"It's just such a stupid thing to do," she moaned. "If they cleaned the floor, they cleaned the closet."

"People make mistakes," James said. "Let's go find out."

Lexie wiped more tears away as she nodded.

CHAPTER 19

Nearing the bottom of the valley floor, Lexie and James stopped at the same time.

James held his finger to his lips, indicating the need for silence. Lexie nodded and made her fingers into a person walking. James nodded. Lexie pointed back up the hill toward the school campus. James shook his head.

James bent down and picked up a pair of fist-sized rocks. It could be Espiranzo, but then why hide? Not to mention that James had worked hard at leaving the Bricks in secret.

Lexie grabbed his arm, trying to stop him. James

shook loose. He wound up and threw a fastball in the direction of the sounds they'd both heard. The rock splashed across leaves a good distance away. James threw the second rock, on a slightly different angle. He hit a tree somewhere in the dark.

Two more rocks, Lexie trying to hang on his arm to stop him. James waited, arm cocked and ready to throw. One minute. Two.

A crackle of leaves.

He threw.

Thud. Might have been a tree. Might have been a person. Quick steps now. The spy retreating.

"James!" Lexie spat harshly as the boy took off into the woods at a full sprint. "No!"

But James was gone, and whoever was in the woods knew it, taking off at the same moment. James galloped through the brush and twigs and deadfall. The spy was heard briefly—a fast runner.

Then silence.

Total, bone-shattering silence. Lexie wanted to cry out for James, but she didn't want to shout a name and didn't want to broadcast that they'd separated. She shivered out of fear and fear alone. Five minutes. More, maybe.

James reappeared up the road, coming down toward her. Shaking his head in disappointment.

"Lost him," James said. He walked past Lexie

and waited for her to catch up.

James didn't speak. Lexie didn't speak.

Lexie finally braved a few words. "Shouldn't we go back?"

"Do what you want." Angry. Mean-spirited. He'd meant to catch the spy. What then? she wondered. What would he have done?

She saw the dirt on his hand from where he'd held the rocks.

What would he have done? she wondered once again.

CHAPTER 20

STRAIGHT UP THE OBSERVATORY STAIRS. JAMES keyed open the door. Marched across the echoey cavern, passing the metal grate stairs leading up to the gray telescope. The room was dark and mysterious. Lexie looked on from the doorway.

James approached the closet door. He didn't look back at her. He was only interested in the door. He tried his workshop key and quickly grew frustrated when the door failed to open.

Lexie crossed and met up with him. She bumped him with her hip to move him aside and took hold of the key herself. She withdrew it. Inserted it, a small distance at a time. As she did, she attempted a gentle turn to the right. The key wasn't quite all the way in when it turned and the door came open a crack. She stepped back.

James snorted, upset with her for succeeding. He took hold of the doorknob himself. Pulled the door open slowly.

Neither spoke.

It wasn't a closet.

CHAPTER 21

A SMALL LANDING LED INTO A DARK HALLWAY.
No windows. Stone walls. It felt like it was underground.

"It's clean," Lexie said.

"Meaning?"

"It's not all dirty and dusty and filled with spiderwebs."

"That's good, right?"

"Not necessarily," Lexie whispered. "It means
it's being used."

"The club probably stores stuff down here.
Come on."

But Lexie caught hold of James as he stepped down. She shook her head violently. The only light came from blinking computer and equipment lights. The air was gray and gauzy. Lexie's head was going like a bobblehead doll's, but left to right.

James held up his hand, signaling for her to stay.

"As if!" she whispered.

James pointed her to the observatory door. "Go. I'll be out in a minute."

"No chance! Wait one second!" She crossed the observatory and shut and locked the entry door.

Together, they headed down the steps.

James took out his phone, about to use its light.

Lexie slapped his hand and slipped out a penlight with red theatrical gel over the beam—the same trick she'd used earlier. It provided a dim light, but enough to see a few feet ahead.

The tunnel was a little longer than a three-car garage. Five feet wide, just enough for two people to walk side by side. Seven feet tall and therefore claustrophobic. Smelled sour, like a mildewed basement. No stairs at the other end, just another door.

Lexie shined the dull red light onto her face. She shook her head.

James frowned. Since chasing the spy, he'd lost all humor. Abruptly, and without explanation, Lexie found herself afraid of him. He gave off a feeling of recklessness, like a boy jumping up onto the railing of a bridge over the river and you really couldn't tell what he was thinking, but you knew somehow he would jump no matter how dangerous it might be.

James wasn't listening. That was it! He didn't care what she thought. He didn't care if she turned around and left him. He didn't care—period. He was Diego on a scent. She lacked a leash. She lacked any commands to control him.

He was going to jump no matter how hard she argued for him to climb down.

James took her by the hand, and for a moment she thought he'd softened. But then he trained the red beam behind them, down the long corridor they'd just traveled. It took her a moment to see it.

A smear. A trail left by a wet mop and blood. She felt slightly sick. A wounded Mr. Lowry had come through this tunnel, through the observatory and outside. He'd been bleeding. He'd been shot.

On the other side of the door they now faced.

"Please . . . let's go back." Lexie was terrified.

James turned the handle.

The door at the far end of the hallway opened. It was a cluttered, filthy basement. When Lexie failed to move, James took the penlight from her and let go of her hand. She snatched back the light.

The school owned the observatory, so technically this was part of the school. Therefore, technically, it wasn't trespassing. More like exploring.

The point was: James was determined to know more, and Lexie wasn't going to let him go alone.

She leaned forward, pushed the door open further, and whispered into his ear. "You first."

CHAPTER 22

THE POINT OF THE THEATRICAL GEL ON THE penlight was to soften and limit its light. The result was its casting a red glow only a matter of feet in front of Lexie and James. The items in the cluttered basement moved and shifted with the dull shadows, causing both kids to twitch and react. A tall lamp seemed to have arms that moved. A chair appeared to walk itself across the floor. Tucked into the beams overhead, nests of cobwebs fluttered with the movement of the children below. James freaked out as an unseen, dangling spider found his shirt and walked up the back of his neck.

Lexie trained the light onto the dusty floor. Whether it was the red of the light, or the dust, or all the junk lying around, there was no sign of a blood trail.

"There's nothing," she whispered. "Turn around?"

"Stairs," James said.

The light caught the wooden staircase that cut the basement in two.

"I've seen too many horror movies," Lexie said.

"You and me, both."

"You can't possibly be thinking . . ."

"We've come this far," James said. "It's not like we have a choice."

"How did I know you were going to say that?"

James took the light from her, and the lead. To their great relief, the stairs did not creak or groan. No hand slapped over their mouths and dragged them off. No cold wind fluffed their hair. They reached the top. James put his ear to the door.

"This is such a bad idea," Lexie said.

James opened the door a crack and peered out. Together, they tiptoed into a hallway just off a small kitchen. They'd entered a fancy home. The space was so unexpected given the look of the outside. Lexie stood still, taking it all in. James motioned above them and play-acted someone sleeping. Lexie got the point. She turned back toward the basement stairs. James turned her around, shaking his head.

James had other ideas. He slipped off his sneakers and had Lexie do the same. They left both pairs on the top stair of the basement staircase.

Quietly, they continued into the living space. A front vestibule, a sitting room to one side, a dining area on the other. The small spaces suggested a husband and wife or even someone living alone. A caretaker? There was no sense of family. No evidence of children.

James tugged on her shirt. They moved through the sitting room and into a small, wood-paneled study. James breathed heavily, racked by memories of the Beacon Hill home. A large desk and a credenza behind it took up a third of the room. James and Lexie moved to the clusters of framed photographs atop the credenza. James aimed the penlight's red beam.

Lexie gasped.

CHAPTER 23

A ROUND, SHORT MAN WITH A STUBBLE OF white hair and eyes with bags, Mathias Hildebrandt was in all the photographs. He obviously liked looking at himself.

James removed his phone, turned off the flash, and passed the penlight to Lexie. Photo by red-tinted photo, James took photos of the photos. Thankfully, many were labeled.

Presidents. Senators. A supreme court justice. Football players. A football coach. A crowded press conference at the White House, Hildebrandt behind the lectern. Hildebrandt at the FBI holding up an award. On both walls to either side of the desk hung wanted posters, awards, documents, and graduation certificates. The life and accomplishments of a career FBI agent.

"Over here," Lexie whispered.

James joined her, aiming the light onto what, even given the red glow, was a yellowed newspaper article. The article was framed. It was captioned in cursive handwriting:

Cape Cod, 1962.
My First Interest in Law Enforcement

James's throat tightened. "Wait a second . . ." he croaked.

"I know this article," she said.

"No way."

"I do, too! My grandfather . . ." Lexie's voice trailed off. "Not that I ever met him. But he was some kind of witness. He disappeared."

"This robbery? You're sure?"

"Positive. My father had a different article, but the same crime."

"What?" James whispered.

She said, "My father kept a photo album of all the newspaper articles that had to do with this. It was a money truck robbery. Millions stolen. They never found the money," she said.

"Yeah . . . I know. I can read." James also had an image of an old pistol stuck in his head. A pistol hidden in a secret drawer in his father's desk.

"Hildebrandt would have been a kid in the 1960s, if he was even alive."

"Maybe not. Depends how old he is. Doesn't help us with Lowry," James said.

"You think he was shot here?" Lexie gasped.

"Or he came here for help. Hildebrandt is clearly connected."

Floorboards creaked overhead.

James glanced around the office. They needed more time.

"Ja—"

James slapped a hand over Lexie's mouth. He signaled her to the door. *Out!* his wagging hand told her.

Lexie took off running. She was into the vestibule before she realized James had not followed. She slid to a stop in her socks.

She heard someone moving upstairs.

She slipped through the cellar door, grabbed her shoes. Moved James's sneakers to the side.

Down into the dark, the red light leading the way. Across the cluttered floor and into the tunnel. She stopped to shove her feet into her shoes.

She ran, and ran. Into the observatory. Out the door and onto the path.

Running hard. Ears alert to sift through all the night sounds. Glancing back, hoping to see James. Her feet continued moving. Her heart racing. Her breath shortening.

And there, among the trees, someone tall. Someone looking out at her.

Lexie screamed. And ran.

CHAPTER 24

WITH BREAKFAST OVER, CLASSES WOULD BE starting in the next hour. Typically this was a time students spent cramming on the homework they'd neglected; others hung out in the common room or dorm lounges.

Lexie and James took a walk. He told Lexie about hiding in the chair space under Hildebrandt's desk, how the man had never come into the office, how it had worked out okay, but that he hadn't gotten back to the dorm until 4 a.m.

Lexie spoke of the figure in the woods—the "spy," as they'd called him. Whose spy? they both wondered. There had been no attempt to hurt them. Only to watch them. Why? Espiranzo had no reason to keep it secret, and James had asked him directly.

Later, James headed toward the chapel. Lexie watched him go, wondering what he was up to. James had perfected the art of lying, a skill that made him an unreliable friend. She wondered if his lying was getting worse, or if she was just getting better at recognizing it. Both possibilities filled her with a certain amount of unease. If he was lying more, that was bad; if she was understanding him better, then was she becoming too close?

James had spotted one of the chapel's two door lights out, recognizing the signal left by Espiranzo. James waited on the far side of the chapel. Once Espiranzo judged the rendezvous safe, he would approach. If he didn't show in the first ten minutes, James was to leave.

Posing as a maintenance worker, Espiranzo rounded the far corner at the five-minute mark.

"Was that you in the woods? I know I've asked, but I need the truth."

"I am sworn to the truth."

"That's not an answer."

"It wasn't me. It should have been me. I am supposed to protect you. Please, no more of the hiding."

"Yeah . . . well . . ."

"I have the information you requested."

"About Hildebrandt?"

"Yes."

"Let's hear it."

Espiranzo studied the area thoughtfully. "If I break off this meeting, don't follow. We'll find another time." James nodded, a rush of heat running up his spine. "Early on, as an FBI agent, Hildebrandt was assigned to organized crime. He ended up busting a bunch of Scowerers, our people. With each success, he rose higher in the Bureau. We used methods to discredit him. We made it appear he was a member of the occult. That he worshipped the devil. He was disgraced. Pushed into an early retirement."

"But he's part of the Directory now!" James complained. "How's that possible?"

"Leverage. He left the Bureau with a good deal of evidence against us, evidence he'd not yet turned over to the Justice Department."

"Why? Why wouldn't he do that?"

"I don't have an answer, except to say that it seems pretty clear he blackmailed his way onto the board. Threatened to bring us down."

"But why? I'm not getting it," James said.

Espiranzo's nervous habit of checking all

around interrupted the flow of discussion. "I'm not on the Directory. I couldn't say."

"You could say. You just won't."

"Speculation. Rumor."

"I'll take whatever you have."

"It may prove false," Espiranzo said.

"I'll keep that in mind."

"It could be that he came to realize he would not, could not, bring us down. That he could not only profit by joining us, but use us, push us in directions the Directory had intentionally avoided for a long time. Generations."

"Such as?"

"Not for me to say."

"Ways my father objected to."

Espiranzo said nothing.

"Lowry, too?"

"Mr. Moriarty, sir—"

"I have evidence. I've followed Lowry's blood trail."

"What's this?"

"To the school observatory." James hesitated, debating how much to share. "Are you . . . does the Directory know that Hildebrandt lives in a fixed-up part of that ruin over there? Across, on the other hill?"

"He keeps a retreat there he uses rarely. His

home is in New Haven. The Directory allows this. It was your great-grandfather's estate. The Directory restored an apartment."

"What about his time before the FBI?" James said. "Earlier."

"I wouldn't know."

"Can you find out?"

"It's possible, I reckon."

"Find out. Where he was born. Raised. School. Who he hung out with."

"I will try."

"Soon. I need it soon!" James then apologized. He rephrased his request. "I'd appreciate that information as soon as it works out for you."

"Understood." Espiranzo stepped closer. "How is it you avoided me not once, but twice? I watched your dorm all night."

"I'd rather not say." James swallowed dryly. He wasn't going to lie to Espiranzo.

CHAPTER 25

THE NEXT WEEKEND, I WENT TO THE CAPE house with Lexie and my roommate, Natalie. James said he was coming, too, but at the last minute he changed his mind and headed to Boston, saying he'd make it to the Cape by dinner. That meant Natalie, Lexie, and I had to go to Lexie's parents' summer house nearby in West Dennis, where a house sitter could "watch" us. So demeaning to have babysitters at our ages. If brothers were born to make sisters angry, James was doing his best.

James arrived at our Beacon Hill home by bus and taxi, kissed Lois hello, and said he had an errand to run. Lois pointed out he'd made her late to the Cape. She offered to take him in order to speed things up.

James declined.

If brothers were born to make guardians angry, James was doing his best.

"You will tell me exactly where you are going, young man. And you will allow me to follow your phone, or you're not going anywhere."

James calculated how to satisfy Lois's control-freak impulses, while still doing what he had to do. "Yes, ma'am."

One of the troubling changes in my brother was that he didn't seem to care about how other people felt. I didn't understand the change. I didn't want to admit to myself it was happening. I couldn't bring myself to face that my brother was hardening into a selfish, unsympathetic crea-ture—not even a human being, but a creature. The evidence was there. Actions *do* speak louder than words. But when you love someone as much as I loved my brother, you make excuses for the other person, you tell yourself it's only a momentary change, that of course it isn't permanent. The more they lie to you, the more you lie to yourself. Pretty soon it's like a pair of tangled earbuds.

James hurried around the house. His room. The kitchen for a snack. The basement. The library. Lois couldn't follow him around like a mother hen. Instead, she waited in her small office off the kitchen for James to tell her when he was leaving and when he'd be back.

"Coffee shop. Library. Back. And then to the Cape. OK by you?"

"Off you go," she said, giving him twenty dollars and reminding him to use his ride-sharing app, not the city taxis.

Lois kept a computer window open allowing her to watch the movement of James's phone. He stuck to his plan. At one point the location software put him on the other side of the wall from the coffee shop. But that wasn't too surprising. The software was far from pinpoint accurate.

James arrived at the jewelry store counter, trying to look taller than he was. The woman was younger than Lois, but old enough to be a mom. Her hair was brushed thin, her makeup overly applied.

"May I help you?" Her voice sounded like air leaking from a balloon.

"I'd like to see the manager, please."

"I can help you. Would you like to purchase or exchange?"

"Exchange, please. But really, I'd like to see the manager."

"That's fine." She sounded horribly condescending. "Allow me to collect just a little more information, if that's all right?" She didn't wait for his answer. "What metal is it you would like to exchange and in what quantity?"

An annoyed James reached into his sagging jacket's right pocket and hoisted the item onto the high counter.

A kilogram brick of pure gold.

Father's treasure.

James, Sherlock, and I had discovered a hidden room off Father's office containing fine art, ornate jewelry, and dozens of heavy gold bars, each worth a fortune. Some of the valuables, including much of the gold, had paperwork to prove its authenticity.

Several months earlier, fearing the treasure might be stolen, James had told me to move it. To hide it. James being James, he'd also advised me *where* and *how* to hide it—no easy task. I'd done as he'd asked.

The woman pursed her lips, clearly believing James was showing her a replica of a gold bar, not the real thing. "If I may?" Her eyes darted between the gold bar and James. "Hmm. We will of course need the—"

James produced paperwork accounting for the purchase of far more gold bars than this one. It had been cataloged along with all of Father's treasure we'd found.

"If you could wait a minute, please? I need to get the manager."

"That's what I've been saying," said James.

The manager, a Mr. Clarence Offel, wore a poorly pressed shirt, a thin tie, and a sour expression. He, too, studied the bar, including the writing that was stamped into it. He read the receipt. He typed something into the computer.

"And you are?" he said.

"Growing a little impatient," James said. The man smirked. "I am the owner of the bar. James Moriarty. It was left to me by my dead father, and I want to sell it to you. For money. Cash."

"Are you aware of the value of this bar, James Moriarty?"

"Thirty-seven thousand dollars. Give or take."

"Give or take. Yes. Correct. You are a minor. You must be eighteen years or older for us to do business with you. I apologize. We also must report any sale resulting in the payout of over ten thousand dollars cash to the Internal Revenue Service. Such a transaction as the one you request would most typically be executed in the sum of nine thousand dollars cash, and the remaining balance deposited by wire into an existing account or brokerage. A certified check can also be issued by our bank in that amount. Do you understand?"

"You're saying you won't do this for me."

"Allow me to make a call. It won't take but a minute. I will need some form of photo identification."

"My passport." James produced it.

"Excellent. I won't be but a few minutes. Please, have a seat."

James didn't want a seat. He wanted thirty-seven thousand dollars. He'd considered sawing off a chunk, but that seemed destructive and maybe even stupid, so he'd brought the whole thing. He now wished he hadn't.

He waited. And waited. Twice, the woman

behind the counter told him it would be any minute.

"I'm on a schedule," James said the second time the woman called over to him through the nasal-sounding speaker. She grinned, apparently getting a laugh out of that.

The teller buzzed the front door open. Lois walked through the door.

"Oh," James said.

Lois stared down at the boy disapprovingly as the manager appeared from the back room.

"This is the last time I'm doing business with you," James called out to the teller and manager.

Lois walked James outside to have a chat. They got through the "What is the meaning of this?" as well as James's answer. They found their way into a heated argument, during which James refused to tell her where he'd gotten the bar and reminded her that she was only his supervising guardian, not his *legal* guardian—and only because first his father and now Mr. Lowry, his legal guardian, had died. On top of that, he needed the money—admittedly, not all of it at once—to carry out what he termed "research," and to make a donation to the school's theater department for an upcoming play the school was putting on.

"Two thousand, now," he said. "The full amount gets split between me and Moria. The lawyers can keep whatever is needed to pay taxes. My one condition: we don't tell Moria. Not now. End of summer, sure. But not now. When she gets curious, bad things happen. She can't know."

Lois looked like she looked when London or Bath spilled the kitchen trash and spread it all over the floor. "You will make no conditions, young man."

"Fine. Then I'm going to request a new guardian."

"No, you're not." She sounded a tiny bit concerned.

"Lois . . . this is about Father. You need to help me. That's as much as I can tell you."

He might as well have punched her in the face.

"Don't think for a moment any law firm is going to hand a fourteen-year-old thirty-some thousand dollars."

"I only get half. Two thousand right now. It's your decision, Lois." James offered her the same look he'd given me recently. A look that reeked of darkness and brooding. A look that warned of a different *creature* within. I knew how gut-wrenching that look could be. It told you he meant what he said. It told you he was ready for what you might throw at him. More importantly it was a look of warning, and one to take seriously.

An hour later, Lois and James sat down at our family bank, where the manager treated the Moriartys like VIPs. Two accounts were opened, one for me—Lois and I needed to sign some forms later. In addition, James had a bank check made out to the school for a gift of one thousand dollars. To Lois's stern objections, he left with the remaining cash in a small envelope.

"No alcohol. No drugs," Lois said, once they were back in the car. "No cigarettes."

"Please! I already promised."

"Again."

"I promise. I swear. I would never ever think about that sh— stuff. My mother was on drugs, right?"

"We don't know that."

"She walked out on us. She couldn't have been normal."

"There's no reason to think drugs were involved."

"Well, anyway, I hate drugs. The money's for some stuff I want. Electronics and computers. You know how expensive all that is."

"Your trust will buy you computers, and you know it. Cash? If you misspend that money, if you lie to me, I will send you to military school just as your father threatened. I wouldn't be too confident that that's not in his will somewhere," Lois said.

James shut up after that. An hour later, he was staring out the window as they drove to the Cape. He couldn't look at Lois. *Military school!* Yes, Father had threatened James. But Lois hadn't been in the room.

So how could she possibly know that?

CHAPTER 26

JAMES AND LOIS ARRIVED LATE BECAUSE OF CAPE traffic. Instead of grocery shopping, Lois took us to dinner at a fish-and-chips place on the beach with a view of the ocean. I like the tartar sauce better than the fish, and I like my French fries with vinegar, which grosses out most of the kids at Baskerville. Their loss. What struck me about the dinner was how normal we were. No drama. Some shared laughter. Good food. Gorgeous view. Other families around us. The smell of suntan lotion. It reminded me how dramatic everything was at school, how the real world was just families eating fish-and-chips. How laughter could change things so quickly. Make friends out of enemies. James and I reconnected at that dinner, no matter how briefly. We were "us" and even Lexie and Natalie were "us." Even Lois.

Later, when Lois singled me out to help her make up a bed, I took it as a hint that she wanted to speak to me alone. It might have been the only time I didn't complain about being asked to do something like make a bed.

Lexie was given the Frigate Bird, a room with one of the best views of the water. It was done in soft blues and white linen, seascape art on the walls, and a bathroom tile floor done as a compass. I loved Frigate Bird, but my chosen room was the Starfish and always would be.

The linen snapped as Lois sent it across in the air for me to catch. We began smoothing and tucking.

"I searched your father's fireplace, as you asked."

"And?"

"Only the key. I left it in place."

"Nothing?"

"The key. That was all. Why did you ask me to look?"

"Just curious if I'd missed something. Thanks for leaving the key. It opens a drawer in Father's desk, but it's empty."

"I see."

I suspected Lois had probably figured that much out. She was a curious, if quiet, woman. She had been Father's secretary and our nanny since before Mother had walked out. James and I both knew that she'd cared deeply for Father. She'd taken his death as hard as anyone. We loved and feared her nearly as much as we had Ralph. But where Ralph had been funny and joyful, Lois was more reserved. It wasn't a fault. It was just who she was.

I assumed she was lying about leaving the key in the fireplace, but strangely it didn't bother me. I didn't believe for a second that she'd have decoded everything the way Sherlock had. And even if I was wrong, we'd moved everything of importance from Father's secret room, so it didn't much matter.

"Your father told you about the key?"

"Only that it was there and that it opened the drawer. He was mysterious about it. I was only to open it if he went missing. Strange thing to ask me to do. But of course . . ." I couldn't say the next part. I could barely admit to myself he was gone. To say it aloud was still too difficult.

"Of course," Lois said, knowing what I had been about to say.

"And it's empty. So, it didn't matter anyway."

"I see."

"You look worried."

"It's all so troubling."

"It is," I agreed. "And now Ralph." I hesitated. "Do you think it wasn't an accident?"

"What on earth, Moria? What a thing to suggest. He was driving. The car crashed. Leave his soul be." Lois was also religious.

"It's just . . . I don't know." We were on to the pillowcases. I found them tricky. Lois tucked one under her chin in order to pull the case around the pillow. I was trying to stuff the pillow into the case, but just ended up chasing it around the bed.

"Acceptance is important to resolving our grief. Things happen. Tens of thousands of people lose their lives in car accidents every year. Not one of their survivors can make any sense of it, just as we can't make sense of losing Ralph."

"First Father, then Ralph and Mr. Lowry. Lexie's father. Is that supposed to be coincidence? Do you really think that's possible?"

We were done making the bed. Lois fluffed everything and smoothed the cover a final time.

The look she gave me told me not to ask such questions. Questions she couldn't answer.

"You and James, you're so young. You shouldn't have to deal with any of this."

"Don't leave us, Lois." I started crying. I hadn't

felt it coming. It hit me with no warning.

She wrapped me in her arms and held me more tightly than I could ever remember. It felt so deliciously good. I hadn't been held like that. Maybe ever. Not that I could remember. Maybe it was just the privacy of only the two of us. Maybe it was the thought of losing such precious people so quickly. Maybe it felt as good to Lois as it did to me. But we stayed like that for a long time. Not long enough for me.

I wish it had never ended.

CHAPTER 27

Socks disappear in the laundry. Toilet paper rolls run out unexpectedly. Lids don't fit on plastic containers for leftovers. Keys vanish. Chargers go missing. I had grown used to so many inexplicable inconveniences. The reverse was occasionally true: a missing pair of pants would show up. A deleted file wasn't deleted after all. Something lost would be found.

But how was I to explain a photograph materializing inside my backpack? Starfish is an ocean-view bedroom done in sand colors with an underwater mural on the walls facing my bed. It is cluttered with all my beloved stuffed animals that I was too embarrassed to keep in my room on Beacon Hill, but never would consider getting rid of. A small, simple table at the window and a ladder-back cane chair faced the beach, providing me with a place to write in my diary, something I did more of at the Cape house than in Boston. My backpack sat on the floor next to the table. Zipped up, the way I always left it, because once, a long time ago, a big, hairy spider had climbed out of it, causing me to scream and later to change my underwear. The spider could have been James's doing. But I didn't think he had anything to do with the photograph. Lois, maybe, though I didn't know when she might have managed.

The colors in the photograph had faded to where they looked drawn by hand. It was mostly dark, a disease creeping in from the four corners. Didn't matter, because the action was at its center. A sticker in the shape of a red arrow pointed to a car across the street (or a lamppost, maybe). I had no interest in it.

It was the car in the foreground that intrigued me. The sidewalk and street I recognized as being out the front door of our Beacon Hill home. A younger Ralph stood holding open the car's back-seat door. I sank into the chair as I understood that the other man was Father, the person whose arm he held, Mother.

I gasped. Mother! I dropped the photo. It landed upside down.

Given all the fresh air of the beach house, I found it strange that I couldn't catch my breath. I grabbed hold of the back of the chair for balance, afraid I might faint. Inhaled. Counted to ten. Didn't feel any better, my head still spinning.

A picture's worth a thousand words, I told myself. Photos can be faked. And this one felt so wrong. So staged. Photos don't prove anything. That was Mother and Father. Ralph. It seemed likely Lois had taken the photo. Who else? Had she also left it in my backpack? Why would she do that?

I wanted to tell myself that it didn't mean anything. Except it didn't look fake. It wasn't a copy. It was stamped with a date that made perfect sense, while not making any sense at all.

Mother hadn't sneaked out of the house and abandoned us—as we'd been led to believe.

Father had taken her someplace—the train, the airport? The date fit. Ralph had driven them. And now, only the person who'd shot the photo might have the answers I needed.

It made no sense for Lois to do it this way. Why not show me the photo and explain things?

So, if Lois hadn't left it in my backpack, then who? Why me? Why now?

Where had my backpack been? Who could have gotten into it?

I threw up. It could have been the vinegar. Maybe bad fish. Definitely not the tartar sauce.

My being sick had nothing to do with dinner at all.

CHAPTER 28

WITH MONEY IN HIS POCKET, JAMES SET HIS plan into motion. By paying out small amounts of cash to Thorndyke, Eisenower, and two clever girls, Stacey and Leith, he bought loyalty from a team willing to work with him. Both girls were seniors, and were seventeen. Important to James's plan to install them as spies. Stacey was smart and good with people. Leith had curly blond hair, bright eyes, and bubbled with enthusiasm. She was the best writer in school. James hoped that besides spying she could help him plot his plans.

Over the week following our trip to the Cape,

James and his team spied on the observatory and the old estate where Hildebrandt kept an apartment. They watched from high up in trees where it would be difficult if not impossible for them to be seen.

A minivan belonging to Sugar Maple Cleaners spent two hours in the driveway on Wednesday afternoon. That Friday, Stacey and Leith applied for part-time jobs with the cleaning agency.

In the woods, well past the edge of campus, a hundred yards from the crumbling estate home, Thorndyke discovered a rusted-out, abandoned vehicle in a trash pit dug long ago. The pit also held an ancient washing machine and a clothes dryer, a great many paint cans—some with bullet holes—broken bottles, and an old toilet.

The discovery gave James just what he'd been needing.

At 10:45 p.m. Saturday, on the hill across from the school, there appeared a small flickering yellow light.

Stacey reported seeing what looked like flames in the forest to her dorm mistress, Ms. Panchell, who relayed the message to the headmaster as well as to the proctor on duty.

From a safe spot near the entrance to the observatory, James and Eisenower saw the glow of

Thorndyke's good work. Orange smoke rose from the garbage pit. The fire started small but grew rapidly. It did not, however, jump the rim and spread into the forest—an important part of James's plan.

The boys waited for someone inside the house to see the fire. All that mattered was panic. James was counting on it.

He got what he wanted. Two men dragged a chain of garden hoses toward the fire. Hildebrandt and a driver left by car.

James found Hildebrandt's departure curious. There was no danger to him or the house, so the only reason James could think of for the man to leave was his not wanting to have to talk to firemen and police if it came down to that. Maybe that was because of his celebrity. His was a face easily recognized, having been in newspapers for years. Maybe it was something else. No matter what, James found it interesting.

With all four men accounted for, James and Eisenower unlocked and slipped through the door into the observatory and soon were through the tunnel and into the residence. Under James's direction, he and Eisenower carefully photographed the study.

On their way back out, James noticed an open door in the basement, just before the tunnel. He stopped and leaned into the room. "Check it out."

Eisenower followed. "It looks like . . . a jail cell."

James shot a flurry of photos, his flash going off because of the lack of light.

"Let's book it," Eisenower said encouragingly. "This is freaking me out."

"Shh!" James continued taking photos. "This is exactly what we're looking for."

"It is?"

"You idiot. Planning is the first step toward victory."

"You read that on a cereal box?" Eisenower said.

"*State of Play* video game. Same thing."

The boys shared a nervous laugh.

James led the way down the long tunnel connecting to the observatory. He opened the door a crack and the two boys entered the cavernous space, the telescope looking like a powerful weapon aimed at the ceiling.

The sound of a key rattled the door that led outside.

James froze. He directed Eisenower toward the telescope machinery while James headed to the wall of computers. For such a big space, there were few hiding places. Eisenower ducked beneath the metal-grate stairs leading up to the telescope, pushing himself into the shadow of mechanicals. James pulled out a rolling chair, squeezed himself into the leg area beneath the counter, and drew the chair close. Breathing hard from running down the tunnel, he fought to calm his breath.

The door opened, admitting the night sounds of the forest along with the slapping of shoes against the concrete floor. James watched a pair of black shoes and cuffed trousers hurry past, the shoelaces flapping like wings. Now the knees and the man's waist, and finally the man himself.

He pivoted swiftly in James's direction, as if sensing or hearing him. James held his breath, his heart beating so strongly in his chest that perhaps it could be heard. If the man's eyes trained slightly lower he would easily see James coiled beneath the countertop. The man's head and shoulders disappeared: he was moving *toward* James.

If the guy got close enough and moved the chair in he'd squish James, hurting him to where James would be defenseless. That left two choices: hope the guy didn't see him, or attack first before the guy got the upper hand. James elected to attack, but his muscles refused. Paralyzed with fear, no matter what his intentions, James's body would not cooperate. He was stuck in place.

The man walked *right up* to the chair and stopped. James could have tied the guy's shoes together. He heard something metal *twang*. A thud. The man cursed. He hurried toward the door and, as his arm came into view, was seen holding a fire extinguisher. James believed the worst was over until the guy abruptly stopped and ran toward Eisenower. He put on the brakes and reached for a second fire extinguisher, also strapped to the wall for emergencies. The guy's hand was less than a foot from Eisenower's unruly hair. With a fire extinguisher in either hand, the guy made for the door. A moment later the door thumped shut.

"Sweet cheddar cheese!" said Eisenower. "I thought the dude was going to give me a shampoo."

"Stay where you are. We give him two minutes and then we're out of here."

They escaped through the forest at an impossibly slow speed that minimized any noise. They maintained a view of the fire and the two men working there for as long as possible.

Spraying water on the oil fire had only made it worse. The belching of the fire extinguishers confirmed a second effort. This, as the whine of a distant fire truck pierced the air. The siren pushed the men to work faster. When at last the fire was squelched, Hildebrandt's men headed off into the woods, away from where James and Eisenower were hunkered down.

Once again, the action surprised James. Why were Hildebrandt and his men so determined to keep a low profile? What were they hiding from?

CHAPTER 29

"Did you see it?" Lexie said, bursting into my dorm room barefoot, in pajama bottoms and a tube top. I had on a pair of sport shorts and a Sam Smith T-shirt.

"The fire? No. But I heard!" I said. I didn't want to sound uninformed. It was school, after all.

"The fire? No! It was on the news. Just now."

I was sleepy and a beat behind everything she was saying. "Lexie, I . . ."

"Your laptop." Lexie barged past me, found my laptop on my bed, and handed it to me to unlock the password. I felt like a robot as I did exactly as she asked. I sat down next to her.

"Here. It's posted all over the place."

AppShot, my favorite social media app, showed a photo of police cars on a cobblestone street lit by mock gas lamps. A reporter's face filled most of the frame, along with the logo of a Boston TV news program. The cobblestones and the homes themselves told me it had to be Beacon Hill and therefore somewhere near where I lived.

The message read:

POLICE RESPOND TO A STRING OF HOME INVASIONS. AT LEAST ONE INJURED.

"Lexie?"

"Here," she said, pointing to the extreme edge of the photo. Had my mind wanted to block it out? Was I unwilling to see what was right there? How had a friend of my brother's spotted what I missed?

"That's our house," I said, my voice in a kind of painful moan.

CHAPTER 30

THE PEOPLE WHO SURPRISE YOU THE MOST often become your best friends. Boarding the school shuttle that would take me into Putnam, where I could board a bus to Boston, I noticed Lexie in the next-to-last row.

"Lexie?" I said, sitting down beside her.

"I'm coming with you." She hesitated. "I'm your guest."

"Is James coming?" I asked, believing there had to be a connection.

"I have no idea what James is up to. I haven't spoken to him."

"But . . . how did you know I was even going?" I asked.

"I was with you when you tried calling Lois, remember?" Lexie looked out the window, willing the bus to get rolling. "I'm not a moron. Your house was broken into. Your guardian, who's more like an aunt, who's your only real family besides James, isn't answering her phone. . . . If it were me . . . ," she said.

I put my hand on her knee. It was warm. "Thank you," I said.

"No problem."

Once on the bus to Boston, I told her that I'd asked James to come with me and that he'd declined. "He said the photo didn't prove anything, that police were all over the street. I pointed out our door was open. The policeman's legs are seen *inside* our front door. He went all James on me."

"He has stuff going on," Lexie said apologetically.

"Such as?" When she didn't answer, I said, "This is Lois we're talking about."

"Understood."

"James is all about James," I said.

"He's upset about Mr. Lowry. Your dad. Ralph. Don't be too hard on him."

"It's Lois. Why hasn't she called me back? She

would have called me back by now."

"No one was killed, Moria. All the news reports said the same thing. Break-ins. Robbery."

"Assault. There was an assault," I said. "Given our luck lately . . ."

"Yeah, I get it. But James—"

"Is only interested in what interests him," I said. "Mr. Mystery. Mr. Conspiracy. If he'd stop for one minute and think about someone else . . ."

"I think he's worried about you as much as he is about himself," she said.

"Me?"

"The circle that protects you and James is collapsing, Moria. You can see that, right? James sees that. James is terrified. Your family is wealthy. Sharks come after money like that when it's left to children."

"You think someone's after our *money*?" It hadn't occurred to me.

She didn't answer. She found the mile markers outside the window more interesting.

I didn't dare tell her about the Scowerers and the change in James since his initiation. How he thought he was so cool, how he'd brought a bunch of loser boys into his inner circle so he could play Voldemort. I wanted to blurt it all out. Instead I watched the back of the head of the person in front of me. Black and oily and a skin condition on his neck.

I searched the seat pocket in front of me. Turned out, buses don't have vomit bags.

CHAPTER 31

Lois opened the front door as I was turning the key. Forgetting my own purpose there, I gasped and dropped my backpack. Despite her attempt to hide it with makeup, the left side of her face was swollen and bruised.

The victim of the assault mentioned on the news had been *Lois*.

I threw myself into her arms, tears gushing. She murmured comforting words, welcomed Lexie, and tried to move to shut the door as I refused to let go.

Lois warmed some tomato soup and put out a

plate of crackers and cheese. Lexie and I ate as we listened to Lois recount the break-in.

"It happened so quickly," she began. "I heard something downstairs, here," she said, pointing to the damaged back door. "I was coming downstairs. I turned at the bottom, and that was it. Someone struck me. They sprayed my eyes. Awful stuff! I'll remember that for a long time! Get a can for myself! I don't know how long they were in the house. I must have passed out when he hit me. The doctor said it could be shock. Police, too. Maybe I'll remember. But I haven't so far."

Lexie and I said how terrible that sounded, how we both were so glad it wasn't worse. Lexie asked if he took anything.

"The silver, the family's good silver. I feel so badly about that, dear," she said to me. "The police say they were looking for jewelry as well, up in your father's bedroom. But your mother's belongings . . . Well, they're not kept in the house any longer."

Those words—"kept in the house"—brought me back to what my French teacher called our "raison d'etre." *The purpose of a person's existence*, or in my case: Father's treasure.

The treasure I'd hidden on James's orders. Once again, my brother proved himself brilliant, though in a somewhat criminal way, I suppose.

Having Lexie with me made things all the more complicated. I couldn't show her any of the stash and I couldn't be rude and tell her to stay in the room while I went and checked if it was still where I'd hidden it. I decided instead to take a long bathroom break in the middle of the night.

Tiptoeing down the hall toward the upstairs library, I was reminded of all the chases between James and me in our childhood. We'd spent so many hours either playing hide-and-seek or trying to kill each other for stealing something.

The hair on the back of my neck stood up, stopping me. Call it intuition or a sixth sense, everyone has a panic button of some kind—a flash of heat, a knot in the stomach, a stab of headache, sweaty palms, goose bumps, dry mouth. Mine was the little feathery hairs back there above the bump in my spine. When they stood up like a cat's, my feet stopped, my heart raced. I went bug-eyed.

I spun around, expecting to find Lexie following me and already making up an excuse. "I couldn't sleep, so I was going to get a book." But no one was there.

Spun around again.

Was I imagining a smell lingering? Perfume? Cologne? Some kind of food?

If the hairs on the back of my neck were a reaction to stage one of self-preservation, if my feet refusing to move was stage two, then my complete system shutdown was probably somewhere around stage six. I didn't have time or the mental capacity to figure out the stages in between. I went straight from stage two to "shutdown mode." Brain freeze. Brain fart. System overload. Meltdown.

A ghost. Right there in front of me.

I might as well have been punched in the throat. Not being able to breathe was bad enough. But now I had an air bubble the size of a grapefruit where my voice box should have been.

My knees went spongy. Somehow, all the lights in the house went dark at the same instant. I blacked out.

CHAPTER 32

THE DEAD DID NOT EXIST. THERE WERE NO SUCH things as ghosts. I knew all that. I was not soft in the head. I didn't believe in pixie dust.

When I awoke, I was eye level to the second-floor hallway's two-hundred-year-old wide plank flooring. The lights were back on. No Ralph, thank goodness.

A pair of bare feet with dark purple nails stood before me, looking about as big as two trees.

"Mo?"

Lexie's voice. Lexie's ankles. For a moment, I could have sworn . . . What a relief. Not a ghost after all.

"Hum-goohg-le," I said. (Rough translation.) My voice box, now the size of an average avocado, allowed something to escape.

"You fainted," Lexie said.

"Did I?"

"Were you sleepwalking?"

"Was I?" Dreaming? I wondered.

She kneeled and felt my head. I winced.

"That's quite a lump. Should I get Lois?"

"No! I'm fine." I sat up. The room spun. Lexie turned upside down. A moment later things went vertical again. I took a deep breath. Felt my head. I'd had worse knots than that.

"What happened?" Lexie asked.

"I . . . It was . . ." I reached out. Lexie thought I was reaching for her. She took my arm and helped me to my feet. In fact, I'd been trying to see, trying to explain to myself why I would have imagined Ralph standing there in the hallway. What had triggered such a memory? Was it important I figure out why I had such a vision?

"Library," I squeaked out.

She led me down the hall, now at my side, our arms locked.

"You scared the wits out of me," she said.

"I . . . Do you believe in ghosts?"

"Me? No! You saw a ghost?"

"In here," I said, directing her into the library. I didn't care if I showed her some of our secrets. I needed help. I needed to know if I was seeing what I thought I was seeing. "Shut the door, please, before turning on the lights."

Blinking to try to clear my head, I sank down into one of the two comfortable chairs.

"Bottom shelf," I said, pointing. "That section there. Take all the books off, please."

"All of them?"

"Yes, please."

Lexie looked as if she might try to talk me out of my request. Thankfully, she changed her mind and started laying stacks of books onto the floor.

"James told me about it," I said. "I don't know if he found it himself, or pulled a bunch of nails out or whatever. Maybe Father showed it to him."

"Nails?"

"You'll see."

It took her a moment to get all the books off the built-in shelf.

"So?" Lexie said.

"I need you to look at me," I said. "To look me in the eye."

Lexie's concern ran deep as she did as I asked.

I stood, all by myself, and dodged the piles of books, barely breaking eye contact with her. "No shouting. No squealing. No sounds at all. You promise?"

"I . . . ah . . ."

"You've got to promise. We can't afford to wake Lois. You will never speak of this, unless to me."

"What is it, like a signed first edition or something?"

"More in the 'or something' range," I said. "You've got to promise."

"OK. No noise. Promise."

"Pinkie swear. You'll never tell another person. No one. Not for any reason, even the most extreme reason. Never." I held my pinkie finger out like a hook.

"Seriously?"

"Seriously," I said. "Swear."

She took my finger in hers. "Swear. This is really stupid, you know?"

"I know," I said. "You'll see."

I jiggled the bottom shelf board. It was dark, polished, probably a rare kind of wood. I didn't know much about wood. It was cut so that the front stuck out from the recessed bookshelf an inch or two. I wasn't great with measurements. The little finger of wood to the right matched perfectly with the left finger of wood on the next shelf over. Father had once told us that a good deal of the oldest woodwork in the house had been crafted by boat builders. The upstairs library's floor-to-ceiling bookshelves seemed to confirm that.

"The trick," I said, pulling the shelf gently, "is lifting at the same time. There are these little—" The shelf came free. Up and out. Lexie helped me set it onto the floor.

"What is that?" she said.

"Insulation." The box was filled with clumps of what looked like shredded newspaper or maybe dryer lint. "Old stuff. From a long time ago."

"I think you hit your head harder than you know, Moria."

"It gets messy," I said. "I use both trash pails." I pointed.

Without asking, Lexie retrieved them. I felt a little bossy, but she wasn't complaining.

"What exactly do you mean by that?" she asked.

I delicately scooped out some of the insulation and placed it into the first of the trash pails. I continued, filling the second. Then I pinched the corners of a folded pillowcase that only I knew was there. Carefully hoisting it so that it cradled the gray clumps, I eased the whole mess into the last of the trash pails. With Lexie's help, it went more smoothly than when I'd done it myself.

As we stood, Lexie got her first look inside.

Despite my warnings and her promises, I had to slap my hand over Lexie's mouth to prevent her screaming.

James's hidden compartment held a stack of gleaming bars of solid gold.

CHAPTER 33

THE TWO OTHER SHELVES HIDING FATHER'S gold presented a mystery: a bar was missing. First bar on the left. Lexie didn't know it, but I did, since I'd stacked them. I'd lugged them up from Father's study, quietly and carefully. I placed them. I knew.

Why just the one? I wondered. If you're robbing a house, wouldn't you take as many as you could carry? Even I had managed to carry four at once. A grown man could easily take four times that in his pockets alone.

"Something's wrong," Lexie said, eyeing me. Testing me.

"Maybe."

"What is it?" she asked.

"Let's check the basement first."

Sneaking around one's own house might feel uncomfortable to some. But it was so much a part of my life with James that when I found myself sneaking around for real, it didn't feel like sneaking around at all. It was more a game for Lexie and me.

We made it through the kitchen and into the basement, a dusty old place with walls of large whitewashed stones and overhead, irregular beams that dated back centuries, not decades. Musty smelling and harshly lit by bare bulbs, it held old suitcases, cardboard boxes, shelves with tools, and more boxes. There was a space cut into one wall that had once been the home's coal bin. It still contained coal. The clothes washer and dryer looked like space aliens among all the old stuff. There was a soapstone sink and a collapsible drying rack with a broken leg that lurched to one side like an old man with a cane.

A few of the boxes lay torn, spilling out their contents. Several suitcases had been opened and tossed.

"They came down here," I said.

"No doubt. How did they know about the gold, Moria?"

"What do you mean?"

"No one robs a basement, right? So they were after the gold."

Lexie was too smart.

"I don't know. Only me, James, and—" My throat knotted. "Sherlock. He would not do this."

"But he knew?"

"Knew? He's the one who figured it all out. Without him, James and I would never have found . . . anything."

"But you trust him, right?"

"Trust him? Of course I trust him! What, are you kidding?"

"But if only you, James, and . . . I mean . . . he gets expelled. He's mad."

"No! That's not even close to who he is. No!"

"People do funny things. That's all I'm saying."

"Well stop saying it!" I said.

She looked as if I'd hit her. I apologized. Then she apologized to me.

I worked my way over and around a bunch of clutter to reach the coal bin. Lexie stayed where she was. "Careful," she said, "there's spiderwebs and stuff."

What she couldn't have known, what the thieves couldn't have known, was that I'd put the cobwebs there myself with a package of SuperScary Stretchy

Spiderwebs. A web in the lower left corner, and a smaller one in the upper right. I felt proud that Lexie thought they were real. The one in the lower left served a purpose. I pulled it away, the webs sticking to my fingers.

"I am going to puke!" Lexie said. "You are so brave!"

I said nothing. I reached into the bin, my fingers seeking out—and finding!—a string I'd attached to the bin's near wall. I pulled. It was tight. On the other end, buried under two feet of coal, was a suitcase containing all the jewelry and coins we'd found in Father's hidden treasure room. I wasn't going to dig it out. The cobwebs remaining in place told me it hadn't been discovered. The paintings, some of them rolled up, some framed, had been harder to hide. I asked Lexie to help me move a wardrobe lying on its side and pushed against a wall. Thankfully, the four stretched garbage bags were where I'd left them. The rolled-up paintings were overhead, tucked into a space between beams. Nothing had been stolen. All told, if Sherlock had been right, there were tens of millions of dollars' worth of art and jewelry hidden down here. Confident none of it had been taken, doubtful that the thieves had even been looking for it, I returned upstairs with Lexie.

"Moria, didn't James tell me about how your father installed all this security gear last summer?"

"Yeah, it was kinda weird. But then . . . you know . . . we found all this stuff and it made a lot more sense."

"No kidding! The thing is . . ."

"What? The thing is what?"

"I mean, I'm sure it wasn't Sherlock, but the video . . . you know."

"I'm so stupid!" I said. "Why didn't I think of that?"

"Well, you can't exactly ask Lois to show you the video of her getting beat up. I mean, that's just not right."

My mind was spinning. There was a closet in the short hallway that led to Father's study. It contained the internet and cable TV stuff along with a sound system and the security gear Father had had installed.

"I'm not exactly a wizard with computers," I said. "That's more James's thing."

"Show me," Lexie said.

"The police would have taken them, right?"

"Doubtful. A copy, probably. If it's all digital then . . . Please, show me."

CHAPTER 34

Bᴀᴄᴋ ɪɴ ᴍʏ ʀᴏᴏᴍ, sɪᴛᴛɪɴɢ sɪᴅᴇ ʙʏ sɪᴅᴇ ɪɴ ᴍʏ bed with the covers pulled up, Lexie worked my laptop from a thumb drive that contained dozens of video clips copied off the equipment downstairs.

Some fascinated me. Others I couldn't bring myself to watch, namely the ones showing Lois getting pepper-sprayed and backhanded as she confronted the robber. Lexie studied it all like a scientist. She even took notes in a SpongeBob notebook I had that dated back to elementary school.

"What are you writing down, anyway?" I asked.

"Observations," Lexie said.

"Such as?"

"Do you remember what Lois said about her getting sprayed and everything?"

"I'd rather not," I said.

"I'm not sure you'd want to hear this anyway. How about I just make some notes?"

"The sun is going to come up soon. I think we should just go to sleep." I finally processed what she'd just said. "What do you mean I won't want to hear it?"

"You clearly didn't catch it," Lexie said.

"Catch what?" I asked, feeling challenged. What had I missed that was so important?

"When Lois was explaining it, she said that someone struck her. Then she said, '*They* sprayed my eyes.'"

"Did she?"

"She did. Singular, then plural. You see?"

"Maybe not?" I said.

"Inconsistencies! You'd have to look at the video, and I know you don't want to."

"No, go ahead, show me."

"You sound angry."

"I'm tired," I said, feeling *much* more awake all of a sudden.

Lexie found the security system's video clip and

played it for me. In color, with no sound, shot from a camera mounted over the back door. I found it hard to watch.

A hooded man comes up the steps and rings the doorbell, then pounds on the door. At the same time he's putting some kind of device into the doorknob. The angle of the camera doesn't allow a good look at every last detail. As the door comes open, a message in red lettering appears on the screen. STATION 7: OPEN. The intruder sprays something—obviously the pepper spray. Lois pushes the man. He slaps her hard and she falls. The man steps inside. The frame goes black.

Before I can ask a question, Lexie clicks on another clip. "Check out the time in the corner. This starts six seconds after the last one stopped. Camera's motion sensitive."

Two other guys, also in hoodies, hurry through the back door. The frame goes dark.

"So?" I ask.

"I don't mean this the way it sounds, Moria. Or maybe I do, actually, but I don't want you mad at me about it. It's only an observation. OK?"

"Lexie?"

"Please!"

"OK. I won't be mad at you." It felt a little first grade to me.

"'*He* struck me,' '*they* sprayed.' Her words. But there was no 'they.' *They* didn't enter for another several seconds. She told us it was mostly blank after that."

"Wait a second . . ."

"You promised!" Lexie said, reminding me.

"You're saying Lois lied? She got hit in the face, Lexie! Him, they? What's the big deal?"

"No big deal. Just . . . weird."

"I think you're super tired," I said.

"Then there's this," Lexie said. She opened a document, not a video. "It's the security panel log. So check this out." Her nail was a chipped clear coat.

"What exactly is this?"

"Each line shows new activity. See? Here's the back door opening. Next, motion detected in the kitchen. Then the hallway. Then . . ."

"Father's office."

"First place they went."

"Hmm." We knew they'd stolen our family's silverware and some silver pitchers. How would the thieves have known where Father's office was, and why go there first?

"Right? You're breaking into a home you've never been inside and the first thing you do is go through the kitchen, turn down a hallway, and open a door into the owner's private study."

"That's not right," I said, my throat dry all of a sudden.

"It's not hard to follow," Lexie said. "And check it out: they've spread out."

"Thieves would do that," I suggested. "Check out the house, search the house as quickly as they can."

"Yeah. I suppose. One guy goes upstairs right away. One into the basement. Moria, if you're robbing a house, would you look in the basement first?"

"Ahh . . ."

"And look at this! The *last* place someone goes is clear down here," she said, moving four pages down the log. "It's the dining room."

"The silverware."

"The silverware," Lexie said, echoing me. "The last thing they even look for."

"The only thing they took." I wasn't sure Lexie could hear me. My throat was closed off.

"That's what I'm saying. They didn't come here to steal silverware. They took it—"

"So it would *look like* a robbery." I felt a chill. I tugged the blanket and tipped over the computer by accident.

"Do you see what it means? What it implies?"

"Maybe not?" I admitted.

"The other two robberies," Lexie said. "Down the street."

I must have been more tired than I knew. "I'm not following you."

"Did you ever see that horror movie where the guy kills something like four people on this one street? Really gross!"

"*Kill-de-Sac*?" I said. "I couldn't watch that to the end."

"That's the one!"

"Disgusting."

"But remember *why he did it*?" she asked.

"I told you! I turned it off."

"It's because the second woman he killed was an ex-girlfriend who'd dumped him. He killed the others just to make it all look totally random."

My head hurt. My chest, too, from a pounding heart. "So you're saying the other houses were robbed to make ours look random?"

"The Interpol detective."

"Superintendent," I corrected. "Colander."

"Him. Yeah. Think maybe you should call him?"

"I can't! I'm not about to tell him about Father's hidden treasure! And I sure as shingles don't want him searching the house."

"All you need to do is show him this log. I guarantee you the other houses weren't searched the way yours was. Somebody needs to know this. It might help them catch them. And if they're caught, maybe some of this will start to make sense."

"Superintendent Colander," I whispered, thinking to myself. "He scares me."

CHAPTER 35

JAMES, WHOSE LACK OF INTEREST IN THE NEWS made him a barnacle riding on the belly of society (as far as I was concerned), heard about the string of break-ins on Beacon Hill sometime Sunday. It was probably because Lexie and I had suddenly left school that morning. James didn't like unsolved mysteries. He called Lois Sunday night, gushing with questions.

A moment after the call with Lois, Lexie's phone rang and she retreated into the downstairs library. I headed off to eavesdrop—being the friend and sister I was—but Lois caught me and returned me to the kitchen with her.

Lexie raised her voice several times during the call. "I did not!" "I don't know what you're talking about!" "I wouldn't do that." It didn't take sneaking around to overhear it.

She came out of the library, her swollen red eyes finding me and Lois in the kitchen. She hurried upstairs.

At Lois's insistence, I gave her some alone time, and finally joined her in my room.

"That didn't sound so great," I said, noticing the clumps of tissue on the floor and the box at her side.

"He's blaming me for something he won't even explain. How fair is that?"

Fair? I wasn't sure. But interesting, I had no doubt.

"Did he give you any hints?"

"No. It's like in his head we had this conversation. But it never happened."

"Yeah, that's my brother," I said. "The World According to James."

"How can he blame me for something when I don't even know what he's talking about?"

"Maybe I do?" I said, hoping she might include me in on it.

She shook her head. "No. It's some kind of big

secret. He wouldn't tell me the secret because of course, in his mind, *I already know*, since I was the one who gave it away."

"That's so . . ."

"Confusing," she said, finishing my thought.

"Do you two have a lot of secrets?" I asked. I didn't know where that came from. Sometimes one's lips get ahead of her brain.

There was this something in her eyes. It was like she'd put in colored contact lenses. Her eyes went black for a moment. Black, like the girl in the horror movie whose body's been taken over by the snake the guy in the mask put in her bed. She wasn't evil, but possessed. She wasn't Lexie but some girl my brother had turned her into. Then it was gone. She nodded.

I felt so cold. She wasn't nodding about fun secrets. She wasn't nodding about awkward boy-girl secrets that made you laugh before you could get a word out. These were *unspeakable* secrets, secrets she wasn't about to tell me and we both knew it. That nodding of hers put a thick piece of glass between us. We could see each other, but we were in different rooms. Different spaces.

James's secrets. The Scowerers? His gang of bullies? School secrets?

"Last weekend," I said, my mouth once again

betraying my brain. It was the most recent James Super Secret, his staying up in Boston with Lois while we'd waited on the Cape. "Lois," I said, whispering, recalling her bruised face. "He's freaking out at you because of what happened to Lois. He feels guilty about that. He asked you about her, didn't he?"

There came the dark Horror Girl eyes again. Impenetrable, like black marbles.

"He asked you about her and then he freaked out on you," I said, "because something happened up here last weekend, something James did, Lexie, not you! And Lois paid for it, not him, and he's all freaky because of it."

She threw the tissue box off the bed and crawled under the covers. She turned her back to me. There was that thick glass again.

I wanted to hear her secrets.

She wasn't about to tell me.

CHAPTER 36

WALKING DOWN THE HALLWAY TO BRICKS Middle Two, I'd drifted off into the lyrics of a song that was stuck in my head. When I got like that, I was in two worlds at once. I followed behind Charity Kennedy and Tiffany Randall by a few paces—they were talking about the way DeSaun Campbell looked in a swimsuit. They and I stepped out of the way for a slightly bent, well-dressed visitor, an older woman, an alumnus maybe, with gray hair and a noticeable limp, her face trained down at her feet. Leilani, whom I'd known since the fall, hurried from the dorm bathroom wrapped in two towels and dripping wet. She dodged out of the way of the older woman. The song was still going in my head as I shut the door to my room behind me.

There were any number of reasons I didn't appreciate finding a fortune cookie on my desk. It sat atop a three-by-five index card bearing the computer-printed letter *M*. Chief among those reasons was that I considered my room a private space belonging to just me and Natalie (who denied any involvement, and I believed her). If left by a boy, he was a perv. If by a girl . . . Well, I asked myself, what girl wouldn't write the *M* by hand, anyway?

I crushed the cookie into dust, my emotions getting the better of me. The fortune was folded in half, also computer printed, the paper cut crudely with scissors.

VANILLA BEAN 7PM

My phone read 6:35 p.m., leaving me no time to get approval from my dorm mistress, a chatterbox and stern-fisted overseer. Instead, I changed into running clothes.

I arrived at the corner coffee shop—over a mile from school—out of breath, sweaty-faced, with hair stuck to my neck, and my London "Mind the Gap" T-shirt dark under both armpits.

I entered at 6:54, having proudly run a thirteen-minute mile, something our dogs, London or Bath, could have managed at a slow trot.

I took a booth to try to hide myself. I was used to ordering from the counter, so it surprised me when a guy showed up to take my order.

"Get you something?" He was kind of hunky for a local boy. Scruffy cheeks. Blue eyes.

"I . . . ah . . ." As in: I didn't have any money on me. Duh! Who goes to a meeting in a café without any money? "I forget, do you take Net-Pay?" I pulled my phone out. He told me they did. You gotta love technology. I ordered a banana nut muffin and a cup of Earl Grey tea. I thought of myself as so sophisticated. He walked away. I tried not to look.

A groundskeeper from school entered. He was someone I'd seen James talking to over by the chapel. The way they'd been standing against a side wall, it had felt as if they were trying to be secretive. It wasn't a face I would forget: sharp, dark, handsome like a movie star.

A Scowerer? I wondered, playing detective. A spy? Had he followed me, or was he merely wanting a cup of coffee? He approached the counter, ordered something, and stood to the side waiting. He never so much as glanced in my direction.

In trying to keep my eyes off the man, I let them stray to another table, from where a high school senior, Leith Gaines, stared back at me and waved. I waved back. Had she been in here when I came in? I didn't remember. Why was a Baskerville senior waving at a girl in the third form? Since when? Even sophomores and freshmen didn't exist to seniors. A middle schooler? If she'd ignored me I would have felt better. As it was, I didn't trust her. Was I imagining that I'd seen her and James and Stacey Levin talking in the common room? I couldn't keep things straight. I was losing it. I told myself to get it together.

And I might have, if, after I'd stared at my banana muffin for ten minutes, Superintendent Colander hadn't walked in.

CHAPTER 37

I DIDN'T WANT TO EAT THE MUFFIN, LEST I LIVE with one around my waist. But I'd ordered it. I'd already drunk half the hot tea. The muffin was begging me to at least break off a chunk and taste it. Until Colander had showed up, my willpower had been winning out.

"Hello, Moria." A thick Scandinavian accent. Coat and tie over blue jeans. Brown leather shoes. Smoke-stained teeth. Any man might have worn the same clothes, but Colander turned them European. I wasn't sure how that happened, but I wanted to learn the trick.

"Hello, sir. Detective. Superintendent."

"May I?" he asked. Strange, I thought, since he arranged the meeting, why ask to join. I said nothing. He sat down across from me. He didn't thank me for being on time—since he was not!—and he didn't acknowledge the difficulty I might have had in making it here. Instead, he started talking as if we were in the middle of a conversation. "James is on thin ice," he said.

That did it. I picked a piece off the side of the muffin.

The same waiter arrived. Took Colander's order for a double shot of espresso and an almond biscotti. Definitely European.

"But it's summer," I said, after the waiter left us. Colander didn't get my joke. "Thin ice? Summer?"

"Ah! I see. You don't take this seriously."

"No. I mean, yes. I do. I'm just nervous, that's all. I'm not exactly close to James at the moment. I honestly have no idea what he's doing, if anything. And speaking of honest: I don't think I want to know."

"Of course you do."

"Because?"

"Do you want him getting into trouble?"

"Of course not."

"It's our belief he may have witnessed a serious crime, Moria. A very serious crime. That he may have evidence, in the form of information, he's keeping to himself. What do you know of that?"

"The break-in?"

He looked at me curiously. "No. Something else."

"Then, nothing." I averted my eyes. The man made me feel he could read my thoughts. My vision fell to the muffin, which was so beyond delicious that I wanted to eat it in one gulp. I was about to pick another chunk from it, when instead I lifted it to my mouth and bit a full third of it free.

"He and I have spoken. I want to trust your brother, I really do. Obstruction of justice is a crime carrying strict punishment. I care about James and you. You must know that. He has brought me important information concerning—"

"Mr. Lowry," I said, guessing. It was the only other big event I could think of.

He answered *yes* with his eyes.

"First our father. Then Ralph. Now Mr. Lowry. You see?" I said.

"More clearly than most," he answered. "Others may not appreciate the connection between the three. Might not see it, for that matter. I want to help, Moria. But if James keeps things from me, information vital to my investigation, not only is he breaking the law, but he's ruining any possibility of me solving Lowry's murder. Perhaps even your father's accident."

I stared at him. "So, you agree with me." I wasn't asking. I was telling.

"James *must* share everything with me. Partial sharing will only confuse things for all of us." Colander wasn't going to answer me. Not directly, at least. But I had my answer: James and I (and Sherlock) weren't the only ones!

The last bit carried a different, more menacing tone. Colander was angry at James and determined to get his message through. He added pointedly, "Did you know you could be considered an accomplice if you're found to possess information relating to James's activities? Oh, yes, Moria. So, I suggest you tell me anything you may know about what he's up to. Right now. Before it's too late."

My top teeth hit something foreign in the muffin. If I'd been alone, I'd have spit it out onto the table. *Disgusting!* But manners made me haul it all into my mouth, mainly because the portion I'd chosen was well oversized and rude to begin with.

My tongue performed gymnastics. Amazing muscle, or organ, or whatever part of the anatomy it was, it *told me* the foreign object was paper; it moved the piece of paper to between my cheek and teeth, allowing me to chew the massive piece of muffin while keeping my lips shut. I swallowed. I even took a small sip of tea while the piece of paper stayed where it was. Now what? I wondered.

"Girls' room," I said. "Right back." I wondered if he heard how weird I talked with paper wedged into my cheek. I wasn't about to fish it out in front of Colander. I hurried. I could just picture that it was only a piece of trash, or something else that had fallen into the batter. I was about to vomit as I uncurled the sodden piece of paper.

Washroom. Now.

I found it interesting that I was already headed for the washroom. In fact, it made me reconsider my destination. Big mistake: I had failed to look around after chomping the muffin's foreign object.

Two steps from the doors marked "Moon" and "Whoa Moon"—with a man-faced full moon and a winking woman-faced crescent moon—something, *someone*, grabbed my arm and yanked me into a closet.

I would have screamed, should have screamed, but 1) I still had some muffin in my teeth, and 2) my abductor cupped a hand over my mouth.

I thought: The groundskeeper? Leith Gaines? The hunky waiter?

The door shut.

The light switched on.

Keeping a hand on my mouth, my abductor spun me around.

CHAPTER 38

ALREADY SQUIRMING, I BIT DOWN HARD ON the flesh pressing my mouth. I caught sight of my abductor in the mirror: a boy with a mustache, brown scraggly hair, and heavy-rimmed glasses over dark eyes.

"Ow!" The boy whispered his complaint, something I hadn't expected and something that terrified me all the more. He's done this before, I thought. "Easy, Mo!"

My heel was currently headed to break the arch of his right foot and cause him to not only release me, but limp for the remainder of his life. Two things stopped me: the use of my private nickname, and his whining complaint as if I should know better.

He released my mouth, spun me around, held me by the shoulders.

"Quiet, please!" he said.

Only then did I hear the traces of an accent—a British accent. Only then did I see past the horrible attempt at a mustache. He'd lost weight since the last time I'd seen him—in a London museum.

I felt excited. I felt speechless. I felt like I'd found a long-lost friend. And yet I felt like running.

"Sherlock?"

CHAPTER 39

HIS SMILE SAID IT ALL. NOT THE BEST TEETH, but coy, cunning, and deeply devious. His eyes struggled to appear happy, but did little to disguise fatigue, solitude, and despair. A bad bruise discolored his neck. It was like the sun trying to peek out between clouds of gloom.

"I can see I've frightened you," he said, his accent impressively more American than British. "I'd thought the reference to 'washroom' might tip it for you. Apologies are in order."

Indeed, I should have caught it: not bathroom, not lavatory, not ladies' room, but *washroom*, a decidedly Sherlockian reference. Hadn't I teased him about it once? Oh, those eyes. They made me sad along with them. They made me want to do something to change them, but if seeing me, if reuniting with me, didn't do it in the first place, what hope did I have?

"How . . . why . . . what's going on?" I gasped.

"Food service industry. I'm all buckets and mops. I wash it up around here."

"You're a janitor?"

"If you must be so crude!"

Oh, Sherlock! I adored this boy. I'd missed him. Tall enough to pass for eighteen, smart enough to teach college, I could imagine him using his crafty ways to pass himself off as someone he was not. I admired him greatly for it.

"I'm not complaining, but why did you come back?" I didn't see how he'd explain it.

"Term doesn't start until September. I never was one for the Cornish coast. The lake hills area is more my cuppa, though I'm unfortunately short of friends who summer there."

Lock, as I called him, was short of friends in general, if I had to guess. He'd been a loner during the school year at Baskerville.

"Why here?" I repeated.

"Certain observations, discoveries, and my

general sense of malaise are to blame. The head-master's actions upset me. I'm not one to get upset, if you must know. I will find ways to get back. Most people are also stupid and beneath me. But more on that another time. Suffice it to say I missed James."

"Just James?"

"There's not time for the meeting I'd hope to have," he said, back to his anxious, twitchy self. "Not with Colander here. Are you acquainted with Espiranzo?"

"Who?"

"As I thought. And the pretty girl who followed you in?"

I didn't like him calling another girl pretty—my reaction surprised me. "Leith Gaines?"

"Is that who she is?" he said, stroking his chin. "Of course. She's cut her hair, hasn't she? And with no uniforms for summer session . . . I see."

I had no idea if she'd cut her hair or not, but I didn't appreciate Sherlock knowing such details. "Has she?" I let slip.

"At whose bidding?" he said, adopting his nasty habit of speaking to himself—thinking aloud. "Coincidence, or was she asked to keep watch on you?" I'd learned to stay out of these one-way conversations of his, but also to pay close attention.

"James? I can't see that. Headmaster? Possible. More likely a proctor or another lower-level operator."

"Scowerer?" I should have kept my mouth shut. Thankfully, as was so often the case, he paid no attention to me whatsoever.

"You must elude Mr. Colander, Mo. I'm not asking you to lie. I know you better than that. He's after answers. You have something he wants. Think about it."

"I am thinking."

"'Twas I who left you that fortune cookie," he said.

"You?"

"I know how you adore sweets."

"You could have been caught in the dorms! You were expelled last semester! You could be arrested."

"You worry too much. You passed me in the hall. Did you forget?"

"Did not."

"Gray hair. Hunched? Nearly ran into Leilani Munamunamorra in a towel."

"The old woman?" I didn't like him seeing me so surprised, because I feared it gave him a sense of power over me.

"I considered saying hello, but I didn't want to overplay the role."

Such conceit was something I'd gotten used to. Other kids at the school resented it and held it against him. "I've got to go," I said. "Colander will think it's weird. Why didn't you just call me, or something? How long have you been around, anyway? Why haven't you called before now?"

"Long enough to shadow you in capture the flag."

"You . . . ! It was you who hit the guy with a rock."

"I'm something of a grand master when it comes to the slingshot."

"You saved me."

"I took issue with a stranger confronting you. Don't make it into drama." He paused. "I also followed your brother and Lexie into the woods. They stole Hinchman's dog. Did you know that?"

"The darkroom?" I asked, aghast at everything he was telling me. "Was that . . . ?"

"Wasn't me."

"Swear?"

"Listen," said Sherlock, "I was hoping for you alone. I didn't expect you to draw a crowd. Colander, especially."

"What's he want?" I asked, realizing too late how stupid that sounded, since I was the one in the booth with the man.

"What isn't his," Sherlock said.

"Which is?"

"You don't know?"

"How could I?" I said.

"Took the words right out of my mouth," said he.

"What do *you* want?"

"Explanations. But there's no time. We'll do this again. Wait for my signal."

"What do I say to him?" I felt the tiny, dark, foul-smelling room spinning.

"You talk as much as possible and say as little as possible. Shouldn't be too hard for you."

I punched him.

"Good to see you, too." He opened the door for me and gently pushed me out.

CHAPTER 40

THE VANILLA BEAN CLOSED AT 8 P.M. I WAS PEEK-
ing out from behind a huge oak out back with a
view of a Dumpster and a screen door. I stepped
out to be seen as Sherlock appeared. He did a good
job of not looking surprised.

"I'll walk you back," he said. "You'll be in trouble for being late to study hours. Demerits."

"Worth it."

"How'd it go in there? You didn't stay very
long."

"I played dumb—and don't you dare make a
joke, Sherlock Holmes! I cut through the rectory

and came back and waited for you."

"Resourceful."

"More like impatient. Why did you get me to come here, Lock?"

"First, I lied," he said. "It wasn't boredom. Certainly wasn't a dislike of Cornwall in the summer. I happen to love Cornwall. It was your father's credit cards—the bit James asked me to look into."

"Father buying the train passes." In looking into Father's death, which the three of us did not believe accidental, we'd discovered some unexplained purchases of train tickets. James had asked Sherlock to dazzle us with his brilliance and attempt to try to explain the unusual purchases.

"The same. Yes. The rail passes are sold by distance. Zones. Concentric circles around Boston city center. Your father purchased such a pass. It took some figuring, but by process of elimination using other credit card charges, I estimate he used the pass regularly once a week. Thursdays. Rarely missed a Thursday. It implies a number of possibilities, some of which a daughter should not consider."

"He had a girlfriend," I proposed painfully.

"I asked you not to consider such things. Possibly, yes. Likely? No. There are no other charges—flowers, wine, dinners—to suggest such a courtship."

"Isn't that clever of you to think of that. Medical?" I said.

"I considered that as well. But the best hospitals are in the city. Why leave the city for treatment, or an appointment? Business makes sense. Something to do with the Scowerers, one would suppose."

"You don't sound at all convinced."

"No."

The Connecticut summer night, the sun setting, the birds flitting about, the smell of cut grass nearly overcame the annoyance and the roar of cars driving past. Sherlock kept his head down and a hood pulled up. I'd never known him to shrink like that. It worried me. Who was he afraid of?

"How could you have left me the photo at the Cape house?"

"Was not me," Sherlock said. "Explain, please."

I described in detail the photo of Mother and Father getting into the car. The sticker pointing to a car across the street. Then, I explained it a second time.

"Use Ruby. Her artistic talents. Your photographic expertise."

"You think?"

"The face of whoever's sitting inside the car across the street," he said. "I believe it may be important."

"A face across the street? Seriously?"

"Use your tools. We will see. We need Ruby's talents to fill in what isn't there."

"Like the driver's face?"

"You two can do this."

I considered his suggestion, bothered that it made so much sense.

"And of course you missed the newspaper," he said.

"What newspaper?"

"Score one for me," he said.

"This isn't a competition!"

"Everything's a competition to some degree," he said. "Even walking now. Who's keeping up with whom?"

"You're the fastest walker I know."

"You see?" Sherlock said.

"What newspaper? Where? The common room?"

"In the photograph, silly! You said there's a man on the sidewalk in the photograph, newspaper tucked under his arm."

It was true: I had.

"Show-off!"

"Ruby," Sherlock said. "Your photography. The newspaper."

"A headline!" I said. "You want me to find a headline so we can—"

"Confirm the date of the photograph. Yes. About time, Moria. You're getting soft! A few months ago you'd have solved that in half the time."

A few months ago he and I had been spending part of every day together. A few months ago I'd been happy despite my sadness.

"Come to the Bean when you have something," he said. "I'll know if you were there." He disappeared through a pair of towering lilac bushes, leaving me walking on my own. I knew better than to try to catch up to him.

CHAPTER 41

THE SUMMER FROGS AND SCREECHING INSECTS turned the nighttime woods into a place so impossibly loud that it covered the approach of four figures dressed in all black. The installation of wireless cameras around the crumbling mansion's exterior was being tended to by Eisenower and Maletta, both of whom claimed tree-climbing skills. The battery-powered, motion-triggered cameras connected over a cellular carrier to an app on James's phone, all financed by his trip to Boston the prior weekend.

Stacey and Leith, now part-time employees of Sugar Maple Cleaners, had yet to set foot inside

Hildebrandt's rooms, but had easy access to the company cleaning schedule (thumbtacked to a cork-board in Ginny Lonstadt's kitchen, which served as her home office). Hildebrandt had rescheduled the housecleaning of his apartment to fit his travel schedule. He was currently away for two days.

The cleaning company also included a proper-ty's security alarm code on the assignment sheet for the few homes that used such codes. The assign-ment sheets were stacked between Ginny Lonstadt's four-slot toaster and her laptop on the kitchen ban-quette, so she could properly input the hours her girls spent on each job, and the tasks completed. Since she was typically about a week behind on her paperwork, the stack was not small. Stacey had found two sheets for the Hildebrandt property, the same security code on both.

Once down the tunnel, James slipped through the door and hurried to the keypad panel by Hildeb-randt's front door. He input the code written on his palm and silenced the box. On his signal, two boys and a girl named Claudette followed in behind him. They performed exactly as James had instructed. The boys took photos and shot video while Clau-dette, a toothpick of a girl with straight hair and a stretched face, installed tiny video cameras dis-guised as screws in light switch wallplates. They cost one hundred dollars each. James searched the office more carefully than on his first visit. He examined a paperweight marking Hildebrandt's government service. Several photographs showing the man in the Oval Office with different presidents.

He reached some of the framed newspaper clippings and stopped. One in particular held him. It seemed so familiar, as if he'd seen it before on a different wall of a different office. A different headline but the same photo: an armored car on the side of the road, police everywhere.

Eisenower startled him from behind. He asked some stupid question James couldn't answer. James moved on.

In the small kitchen, he noticed a pad of custom notepaper by a wireless telephone. He tried a trick he'd seen in a movie: rubbing a pencil lead gently across the top sheet to reveal impressions from the note made above it.

avocados

bananas

soy milk

raw sugar

coffee

James hurried upstairs to the apartment's only bedroom. Another custom stationery notepad sat alongside the bedroom phone. James rubbed this as well. Not all the impressions had been made strong enough to carry through.

6_7_ _23475

A_ _ _an_ _ _ _

He raced downstairs to Hildebrandt's office and was in the process of rubbing that notepad as well when, only by blind luck, he happened to check if Claudette's hidden cameras were showing up on the app yet.

A car pulled into the driveway.

Men were getting out of the car.

James sent a group text:

> code red

Maletta and Eisenower hurried into the kitchen and headed into the basement. James skidded to a stop as Claudette dropped a small switch plate screw onto the floor, electronics hanging from the wall. He couldn't leave her.

"Thirty seconds," he said. "Maybe less." He

tapped some keys on the security panel. It started beeping.

"Got it," Claudette said, her voice impossibly calm. She retrieved the fallen screw, pushed the wires into the wall, and put a screwdriver to the screw.

"You and me, up here," he said, from his position by the door. "We won't make it out."

"Just a few more seconds," she said, her feet working to pile up the tools on the floor while her hands finished tightening the screw. She reached down, snagged all the tools, but dropped some small lengths of rubber wire covering—the trash from the work she'd done.

"Now," James said in a whisper as he watched the front door deadbolt move.

Claudette glided across the floor, hands on her tool belt to keep the contents from making noise. She worked on the security panel. It stopped beeping—the alarm was set.

James held the coat closet door open for her. She slipped inside. He squished up against her as he pulled the closet door shut, enclosing them. They were as close together as if slow dancing. It was pitch black. Her hair smelled sweet, like breakfast cereal.

James was hungry.

The alarm started beeping.

The front door had been opened.

Being pressed against a girl was more scary than whoever had entered the apartment, but James managed to overcome the fear by concentrating on the conversation that *didn't* take place. The swish of clothing told him that two people had entered before the door was closed, then the alarm's countdown beeping was silenced. One wore shoes that sounded like a kiss with each step—the same sound made by deck shoes. The other person's pant legs whispered with each stride. Two distinct people, James thought. The two did not speak. Squeaky Soles moved to the left of the closet. Swishy Pants headed farther away. Several minutes passed. James's and Claudette's breathing competed against the other's. Claudette leaned to separate herself from James, but his hand caught her shoulder and stopped her.

"Hangers," he whispered, practically eating her ear through her hair. He'd spent plenty of hours hiding in closets during hide-and-seek. He knew how hangers could clank like bells.

"Clear!" said a man's voice from afar.

"Clear!" returned another man from a different distance.

Squeaky and Swishy were bodyguards. They'd just checked . . .

Quickly, James hugged Claudette even tighter and spun 180 degrees, both putting her back to the closet door and, more importantly, folding the two of them fully behind the hanging coats instead of between them. He squatted down a few inches to bring his head below the closet hanging bar and he placed his hand on Claudette's head and pulled her tightly into the crook of his neck and shoulder, practically smothering her.

The closet door came open . . . and shut.

James had anticipated that if the two were conducting a search of the rooms, they wouldn't completely neglect the coat closet. If he hadn't moved himself and Claudette, they'd have been caught.

Claudette gave James an extra hug to thank him. Neither could breathe, they were so scared.

What now? James wondered.

The sounds told him at least one of the guards had gone back outside. A car door shut. The front door shut.

"Listen, I'm just home now." A man's annoyingly high, irritating voice. "You're what, six hours ahead? Carry on as charged. This only works if they don't see it coming. They won't kill the messenger if they like the message. Get it ready. I need it in place."

Wondering if the software was recording this,

James worked to memorize every word. In case he missed some of it, he whispered for Claudette to do the same. He felt her chin dig into his shoulder as she nodded. He eased up on holding her head so close, hoping he wasn't smothering her. They waited. And waited. Eventually the slice of light at the bottom of the closet door went dark. They waited even longer.

Eventually, James led the way out of the closet, down the hall, and into the basement. He and Claudette moved like escaping prisoners. Minutes later, breathless, they fled from the observatory and into the woods. Claudette took his hand as they moved through the dark. James considered breaking their grip, but allowed the contact.

Reaching a clearing, they both bent and gripped their knees, out of breath.

She said, "I know I'm not supposed to ask . . . I promised not to ask. But who is he?"

"Do you remember what he said?" James asked, panting.

"The last part, yeah, about them not killing the messenger. But who's the messenger, anyway?"

James didn't answer. Wasn't able to answer. Running through the dark woods, he'd been focused on one of the three pieces of notepaper in his pocket. The one with the numbers and a few letters.

Two things had jumped out at him. 6_7 was likely 617, a *Boston* area code. With that tidbit of information, the letters below the number made more sense.

A___an____

became

Alexandria

Lexie was her nickname.

James spit into the grass, allowing Claudette to believe he was simply out of shape.

CHAPTER 42

THE LIVE IMAGES OF HILDEBRANDT AT HIS office desk came from one of Claudette's hidden cameras. James had been addicted to watching all the images over the past twelve hours, nearly getting caught during math class.

Back in his dorm room now, skipping lunch, he grinned, thinking that he was secretly eavesdropping on a man who had once run the FBI and had therefore been in charge of so much surveillance.

He'd also been focused on Lexie's name and phone number being on Hildebrandt's notepad, something that continued to make him feel sick.

The other page was a grocery list that James dismissed as unimportant.

He watched the man dialing the desk phone. James pushed the earbuds in deeper.

"If you can't trick Moria into showing you, then consider something more forceful," Hildebrandt said. He paused to listen. "I understand the friendship," he said, "the trust, of course I do. But this is important information to us!"

James could only think of one person with whom Hildebrandt might be speaking. He speed-dialed Lexie's phone.

It went directly to voicemail.

Lexie's phone was busy. Hildebrandt's phone was busy! If James had harbored any doubts about her number being scribbled onto a phone message pad in Hildebrandt's apartment, they vanished.

Lexie was a traitor?

James texted Claudette to meet him on a bench after lunch. She texted back that she'd be there right away.

Once together, James asked her to recall the words they'd overheard Hildebrandt speak. He had his own version written down and folded in his hand.

"Something about six hours," Claudette said, eyes squinted. "Carry something? What I remember pretty clearly is the thing about 'They won't kill the messenger if they like the message.' Then something about being ready and that he needed it in place."

"Do you remember 'six hours *ahead*'?"

"Yeah," she said excitedly. "That was it! Ahead of what, though?"

"Time change, I think. Not 'in advance of something,' not 'ahead' like that. Six hours ahead. That's Europe. The person he was talking to was in Europe."

"Seriously?"

"'It'll only work if they don't know,'" James recalled. "Something like that."

"'If they don't *see it coming*'!" Claudette said.

"Right! Perfect! That was it. That's it exactly!"

Claudette sat up taller and more proudly. Closing her eyes, she recited. "'I need it in place.' That's how he ended it."

James grinned, writing it down. "I think you're right. That sounds like it to me."

"So who is *they*, do you think?" she asked. "And what aren't *they* going to see coming?"

"And what does it have to do with Europe?" whispered James aloud while he churned over the fact that the Scowerers had both allies and enemies in Europe. As the leader of the Scowerers, he thought he should have known more than he did about such business ties. "Sometimes it seems like your friends are your enemies and vice versa," he muttered.

"Are you describing middle school or high school?" Claudette asked with a grin.

"Both?" he said, glad that she'd misunderstood him. Everything to do with the Scowerers was strictly secret.

"Hey, *you two*!" Lexie was coming up the sidewalk from the common room. She called out to them both, but her accusing eyes were locked onto Claudette. Supposedly, Lexie and James were kind of girlfriend and boyfriend, a relationship James had yet to fully acknowledge.

If James had been honest with himself he'd have told her to get lost. But James the Manipulator, James the Great of the Scowerers, saw things differently. You didn't push away enemies, you got as close to them as possible.

Both Claudette and James said hello.

"I didn't know you two were chums," Lexie said, a little bitterly.

"We—" Claudette said. "James—"

"I hired her," James said honestly. Father had told us dozens of times that "Once a liar, always a liar." He'd schooled us that little lies become big lies, that untangling a lie never works because there's no truth to it to begin with. "Some electronics. Security stuff so that I can see what's coming." He didn't happen to say where or who.

"That sounds cool," Lexie said, looking at Claudette for the first time. She didn't mean a word of it. All three knew exactly what she meant: *That sounds like competition I don't need.* Lexie added, "I see you're taking notes."

James stuffed the note away in his top pocket. "How about you? What are you up to?"

"Lunch?" she said, as if it was the most obvious thing in the world.

Phone calls? James wanted to ask.

"Didn't see either of you in there," Lexie said. "Lunch."

"We lost track of the time," Claudette said, speaking up for the first time. She seemed to be teasing Lexie, taunting her.

Staring down James, Lexie spoke sharply, only to him. "You lost something too." She walked off.

James caught up. "Lexie," he said in a hushed voice, reaching to stop her. "I'm sorry!" She shook off his grip and James knew better than to try a second time. He walked alongside of her. "She's helping me. I hired her! She set up some surveillance equipment for me. She covers Mo, too." He

felt the lies come easily, wishing he could pull out
the notepaper and write them down so he wouldn't
forget them. *Little lies become big lies.*

"So, you're paying people to be your friends
now?" Lexie said. "What about Thorndyke? Eisenower?" When James didn't answer, Lexie stopped
her brisk walk. "You can't be serious! I was *kidding.* You are *paying* those two? That's disgusting,
James! Shame on you! How desperate are you?"
She hurried off, leaving James stuck where he was.

"It's not like that!" he shouted at her back.

Lexie kept on walking.

"It's not about friendship!" He heard himself
speak the words before he thought through their
consequences. Turning back to Claudette, he saw
her face bunch like a shrunken head. "I didn't mean
that like it sounded," James called to her.

But Claudette hung her head, slipped off the
bench, and walked in the opposite direction. James
in the middle, with two girls walking away from
him on either side.

"Oh, great," he said.

CHAPTER 43

CLOTHED IN A FLOOR-LENGTH ROBE OF RICH purple trimmed with gold piping, James descended a stone staircase into the Scowerers' underground chamber behind the school chapel. It wasn't his first time, and wouldn't be his last, but he nonetheless felt a wave of awe and fascination swell at the sight of the flickering torches and candles lighting the earthen floor and root-tangled walls. Overhead, the largest tree on campus stood outside the chapel nave, its crown stretching twenty yards across, its canopy seventy feet high. Beneath, the roots, as thick as small trees braided like a den of snakes. A long table had been placed in the chamber's center, around which fourteen men and women wearing black robes awaited the occupant of the empty chair at the head of the table.

James took his place, his mouth dry at the sight of all these grown-ups staring back at him. He poured himself a glass of water, working hard and winning at keeping his hand from shaking. Headmaster Crudgeon sat to his right, followed by two women, a balding man, and another with a gray beard and grayer eyes. James met eyes with each member of the Directory as Father had taught. He awaited a silent acknowledgment from each, a subtle exchange signaling James's authority. Crudgeon, serving as deputy governor, relied upon years of service to assume the burden of leading the meeting and keeping James from embarrassing himself.

"All Directory regents are in attendance. There will be no reading of minutes, as this is a special council to elect a member to fill the seat of chief advocate, vacated by the recent passing of our dear brother, Conrad Lowry. Do I hear nominations for the post of chief advocate?"

A name was put forward and seconded. Two more, the same. Then a puggish man whom James recognized from the photos on the wall of the estate. It was Mathias Hildebrandt. Shorter than the others, his robe ill-fitting at the shoulders, the round-faced Hildebrandt's forehead shined and his wet lips sprayed spit as he spoke, some of which sizzled in the candle flames.

"I put forth Kennedy Wilkes, Esquire." His overly wide-set eyes briefly searched the members' faces. The other seconds had been quickly volunteered; this one took longer. Ms. Marion Finley finally backed the nomination. Roger Albright, secretary regent, took down the details. "Ms. Wilkes, as you may remember, served as lead attorney in the Brightman case, and is the daughter of Terrance Wilkes, who acquitted both Denny Vedelis and Pietro Gianoglio."

James, having been counseled by Crudgeon for the past two nights running following dinner, had known not only what to expect, but from whom. As with the nominations that had preceded, Crudgeon opened Ms. Wilkes's nomination to discussion.

"You are . . . Regent Hildebrandt," James said, purposely tentative. He wanted to avoid feeding the man's ego, if possible. "If I'm not mistaken," he continued, recalling the exact words Crudgeon had supplied him, "Ms. Wilkes's book, *The Timeline of Terror*, reflects a political and monetary conservatism that might—only might, I admit— suggest a tighter fiscal policy overseas at a time when domestic revenue is decreasing." He glanced to Crudgeon, who signaled him he'd done well.

"I'm sure a fourteen-year-old knows everything there is to know about international jurisprudence and economic policy," Hildebrandt said.

James summoned his considerable memorization skills. "My father, and my grandfather before him, held this society to certain standards," he said. He looked to each of the people around the table for agreement. "I think he called us 'simple thieves.'" James won some nods. "I know he worked hard to keep us from . . . engaging in the business of drugs, for instance." More nods. "We are organized. We are criminals. But we are not organized crime. We don't murder. Torture. Kidnap. There are . . . limits, I guess you'd say."

"And there are opportunities," Hildebrandt said. Clearly, he wasn't alone. He, too, received agreement from the others. "There is progress. I'm not suggesting anything close to drugs. No kidnapping. Do not exaggerate my position, please."

"We're negotiating percentages with our Eastern European partners," James said. "That's hardly a negotiation for a lawyer who sees us pulling out of Europe. Your nominee isn't right for us at the moment."

"There's no such animal as an Eastern European

partner," Hildebrandt countered. "That translates to Eastern European tyrant. We don't negotiate with tyrants. We shouldn't be doing business there."

More heads nodded in favor.

"But, if the Eastern European deal is handled incorrectly, we could easily lose territory and get nothing in exchange."

"You would suggest?"

"I will make suggestions. But they will be to our new chief advocate. When the time comes, a list of options will be put before this Directory." James struggled to keep from looking at Crudgeon for approval.

"You are a child. You should be listening, not talking." Hildebrandt was quickly losing patience.

"The nice thing about being fourteen," James said, "is you don't waste a lot of time shaving. It frees up more time for study."

All but Hildebrandt chuckled.

Hildebrandt talked of his nominee's ability to consult her father and to draw from his experience. "If you have your own nomination, Governor Moriarty, please, let's hear it."

Crudgeon had advised James to be quiet if Hildebrandt pushed for a name.

"I nominate an idea, not a person," James said.

"In honor of my father, I request the society not enter into destructive practices. I think you are suggesting we help terrorists to get money without being caught. You say there is enormous profit to be made."

"Thirty percent or more," Hildebrandt said.

"They kill Americans."

"Not those I suggest doing business with. They are rebels for freedom."

"They are terrorists. Even worse than drug dealers." James leaned on both elbows, his face red. "How could we do something like that?"

Not pleased, Hildebrandt squinted at James. "How?" He was mocking James. "We vote on it?"

Ms. Ewa Latak, an olive-skinned woman with dark hair, served the board as a parliamentarian. "There is no motion to be made at this time. We lack a quorum."

James fought back a smile. Headmaster Crudgeon had talked two members of the Directory into missing the meeting.

"Any other discussion on nominees or other nominees to put forward?" James said. Discussion continued. Board members appeared split on Hildebrandt's nomination. Crudgeon had expected this. He'd also predicted that when the time came, Hildebrandt would get the nominee he wanted.

But James had used his time wisely, had reminded the Directory of the dangers of expanding into international money laundering. He'd exposed Hildebrandt as a man focused on profit, not patriotism.

Crudgeon gave James a slight nod. A tiny smile of congratulations. James had scored points against a man who'd recently been the most powerful law enforcement officer in the country. For now, that was the best that could be hoped for.

A bigger mission presented itself: James needed Hildebrandt off the Directory before the man wrecked everything Father had worked for.

That wasn't going to be easy.

CHAPTER 44

THREE MASSIVE FLAT-SCREEN MONITORS, A LAP-
top, and a high-speed internet connection from a
satellite dish James and Maletta had installed next
to the dorm's chimney, the wires carefully tucked
behind a drain pipe, comprised what James called
the War Room. The gear was set up inside James's
dorm room closet, a place the proctors never
looked, knowing most kids shoveled their clothes
in there in order to pass inspection.

Dressed in underwear and a T-shirt, James sat in
his desk chair with his legs inside the closet, the wall

of video in front of him. The motion-and-sound-sensitive cameras they'd installed in Hildebrandt's apartment recorded hi-def images and sound to four external hard drives. It was James's job to review every video clip, no matter how short or apparently insignificant. Some were sound-only, the camera picking up a conversation in a nearby room. Then, there were the false recordings, mostly of the driveway, when the recording was tripped by a squirrel or deer crossing into the viewfinder. James had to study these as well before discarding them. He'd never understood how time-consuming surveillance could be. Even using fast-forward, it took him over three hours to review a day's worth of captured video. Very few conversations interested him. Those that did, he copied into a special file and also onto cloud-based storage. He left no trace of the cloud storage account on the laptop. The only mention of it existed in a secret email to be automatically sent to me, his sister, if anything bad happened to him.

The sound of the door to his room opening abruptly caused James to immediately yank off his headphones and slide the closet door shut. Standing, he pushed the desk chair back against the wall. James slipped his shirt up, as if just pulling it on, so that as Mr. Cantell appeared through the door it might look as if James was just getting ready for bed.

"Ah, Mr. Moriarty. Glad you're still awake." That was news to James. Typically, the hall master frowned upon students with lights on past eleven, though such rules did not exist beyond dorm curfew. The comment felt like a trap.

"Just going to bed, Mr. Cantell."

"Not quite. You have a visitor. Dorm lounge. Straightaway. Off you go."

"I'm in my underwear, sir."

"Don't be rude, young man. Pull something on. Get going. You don't keep a man like this waiting."

James swallowed dryly. Hildebrandt? He hopped into the legs of warm-ups, and followed Cantell barefoot to the dorm lounge.

Colander! The superintendent sat imperiously in one of the lounge's uncomfortable chairs, looking impatient though not tired. He patted the arm of a stuffed chair beside him, making James feel like a child, so James remained standing. Colander indicated the chair again. James sat down.

"If we might have the room?" Colander said to Cantell, who had followed James. Cantell looked embarrassed as he left.

"I wish I could do that," James said. "Make him go away like that."

Colander smirked. "The power of a badge, my boy. Nothing puts the fear of God into a person like the sight of a bit of tin." He cleared his throat. It didn't help his accent any. James concentrated so as not to miss some words. "You asked me to look into the details of Mr. Lowry's death. I have done so. It was the bullet wound. Two, to be exact. Both to the abdomen. It must have been a difficult sight for you."

"He was lying down," James said, recalling finding the man in the woods. "It was dark. Capture the flag."

"Lucky for you."

"I guess. Not really. Not at all. I've known him forever."

"Such a strange expression coming from someone so young."

"I don't feel so young. Not anymore. Everything changed when my father . . . It's been . . . different."

Colander touched James's arm and James flinched. "We learn to put these things behind us," Colander said. It might have been his accent. It might have been the man himself. But the comment lacked any sympathy whatsoever. It sounded more like the man was reading.

"I'll never put him behind me," James said. "He's with me every day. I hear him. I see him. I don't exactly believe in ghosts, but if I did, I'd say they're a lot friendlier than I thought."

"Hmm," Colander said. "Something of a philosopher, are we?"

"No. Just a son."

Colander turned his head to look at James, but James continued looking straight ahead. "Maybe not so young after all," Colander whispered.

James felt a chill.

"Dirt and debris on his clothing is inconsistent with the area of the street where he was discovered."

"I told you."

"The report suggests he was likely shot in a nearby city park."

"Not true."

"That he made his way some distance and collapsed."

"He made his way from the woods down the hill," James said. "That's some kind of walk, here to Boston."

"Tell me about it," Colander said. "Did you happen to see if he was wearing one shoe or two?"

James felt an air bubble seal his throat. He didn't dare try to speak.

"The police have searched the park for blood evidence and the shoe. Nothing so far. Wounds to the abdomen produce a good deal of bleeding."

"Let me guess," James said arrogantly. "There's no blood trail on the street or the sidewalk or anywhere around where they found him, is there? That's because he was probably in the trunk of a car." James heard himself and was reminded of his former roommate. Sherlock Holmes had left a bigger impression on James than James would admit. He appreciated facts now. He felt confident, even over-confident, when delivering them. He'd hoped to steer the conversation away from the missing shoe. No such luck.

"The man's right shoe is missing. Strange, don't you think?"

"It's probably in the car, too," James said, providing a lie that sounded perfectly reasonable. "Or maybe it fell off when they moved him. Have you heard of a man named Mathias Hildebrandt?"

"The FBI director?"

"Used to be. Not anymore."

"Once an FBI director, always an FBI director." Colander amused himself with that one.

"Do you know where he lives?"

"Haven't any idea. Should I care?"

"He killed Mr. Lowry."

Colander chuckled. "The most powerful policeman in the United States? Or former policeman? Hunted him down in the woods, did he? Here, in

Connecticut, behind your boarding school. I highly doubt that, young man."

"Or one of his guys, maybe."

"Because?"

"I'm working on that."

Another chuckle. "You might want to find that missing shoe. Put those shoes together, you'd have a suspect."

Put those shoes together, James heard. *Forest elf.* Lexie and he had talked about the Brothers Grimm clue, the story about the naked *elves* making shoes for a cobbler. *Putting shoes together.* James tuned out Colander. Tuned out the dorm. He put himself back in the woods with Lowry. Back with Lexie talking about the meaning of the fairy tale. Lexie saying how the story didn't have much of a moral. He thought about his former roommate's way of flipping pieces of evidence around and building one thing out of others. "Putting shoes together" became "taking them apart." A pair of shoes became two individual shoes. Separate shoes. James could taste the truth of the thing. He nearly had the answer right there in front of him. But it was like trying to swipe a fly out of the air. To catch a mosquito and squish it. *Putting together. Taking apart.* Separate the shoes. Take them apart.

There it was. That thing. That perfect gem of

an idea caught. Captured. His!

Take the shoe itself apart. Whatever clue Lowry left him was built into the shoe.

"Whoever has that shoe is the killer," James heard Colander say, having no idea what he might have missed.

"What? No!" James protested harshly. The shoe was in his dorm room. "I mean, yeah. I suppose. But not necessarily, right? I mean, who knows where it fell off? A groundskeeper could have found it, I suppose. A student." He tried to swallow. "Maybe it's still out there." James was already forming a plan to put the shoe back into the meadow where he'd found Lowry.

Colander looked at James sternly. "Possession is nine-tenths of the law," he said. "That shoe will point to the killer."

"Maybe," James said, thinking that it might point to the killer in ways Colander had no idea of.

"Let's just say I believe you now," Colander said, "about the body having been moved. The evidence does support it. Or lack of evidence, I should say. I'd like you to show me where you say you found him."

"To look for the shoe," James said, though his voice cracked.

"To look for the shoe," Colander said. "But with no one the wiser. You understand? Tomorrow afternoon? I could meet you down at the hockey rink."

"I might be busy tomorrow afternoon," James stuttered. "School's getting harder right now."

"Is it?" Colander didn't trust him. "Interesting."

"I'll call you," James said. "If not tomorrow, soon."

"Tomorrow," Colander said. "I don't have to remind you, a man was killed."

"No, you don't have to remind me," James said.

CHAPTER 45

JAMES FOUND THAT WALKING CALMLY IS A CHAL-
lenge when your heart is racing. All he had to do
was leave the dorm lounge without looking suspicious, without stirring Colander's curiosity. It took
all his concentration to pull it off.

Back in his dorm room, he breathed for what felt
like the first time in minutes. Naked elves. Shoes.
How had things gotten to this? he wondered.

His patience tested further, James sat on the
edge of his bed for another ten minutes in case
Cantell or Colander pulled another surprise visit. If
only the dorm rooms locked. He briefly considered

moving to a bathroom stall, which did lock, but he needed a hard surface like his desk. This, in turn, led him to realize he would need tools—cutting tools, gripping tools, the kind of tools found in what students called "the steamer," technically, the Multidisciplinary STEAM Makerspace.

It being late, James stuffed his bed to look like a boy was sleeping and left through the window.

The steamer, not far from the gymnasium, occupied the entire ground level of the science building. It included the lab, a robotics area, wood shop, and metal shop as well as every kind of workbench, tool, and device, from a 3D industrial printer to an arc welder. The photo and video lab was closest to the makerspace's main door. James set up on a wood shop bench, working in the red light of one of Lexie's gel-covered flashlights. The flashlight's batteries were running low, causing him increasing anxiety.

At last, he sensed Lexie and me standing a few yards behind him.

"Cheese-Its! Cripes!" he exclaimed. "What the hello are you doing here?"

"Moria saw you heading down here," Lexie said. "She texted me."

"The whole school would have seen you if they'd happened to be looking out their windows," I said.

"If you want to sneak into the steamer, James, you might avoid crossing the JV field out in the open."

"I was in a hurry," he said, as if that was any kind of excuse.

"To shine a shoe?" Lexie said, knowing perfectly well it wasn't his shoe.

"Colander," James said. He explained the meeting with the superintendent, though not the reason for it, and how he'd come to think of Lowry's shoe differently. "The elves, the naked elves, built the shoes for the shoemaker while the guy slept. They put them together. So what if Lowry was telling me to take them apart? *It* apart," he said, indicating the lonely shoe on the workbench.

We joined him at the workbench.

"The heel's the most obvious," Lexie said. "Did you check for a pin hole? Someplace a paper clip could be inserted?"

"Who are you?" I said.

"I saw it in a movie," Lexie said. "This spy used a paper clip to unlock the heel of his shoe and there were these codes inside."

When we failed to find any such trigger, James tried twisting the heel, pulling on it. Finally, he used a chisel and hammer to remove the heel. Nothing but chunks of wood, rubber, and leather.

Next, with Lexie and me holding the shoe

steady, he separated the sole of the shoe from the leather uppers. No hidden space.

Lexie came up with the idea of running ultraviolet light over the shoe, because she'd seen another movie where the light revealed hidden codes. Nothing.

"Before we destroy the thing entirely, and maybe the secret message with it—if there is one— what about we think this through?" I suggested.

They looked at me as if I'd passed gas.

"Put ourselves in Mr. Lowry's position," I continued. "He's hiding something for others to find. Maybe it's a note. Probably a note."

"So he has it sewn into his shoe," James said, impatience weighing on him. The flashlight flickered, dimming. "Duh! That's why I'm taking it apart."

"It's not a note," Lexie said. "A note could get wet and hard to read."

"So, it's in plastic," James suggested.

"Maybe."

"Or?" I said.

"Waterproofed," Lexie said, nodding, "that's important. And easy to get to. But not a note."

"It's in the tongue," I said, guessing. "It's one of those small memory chips, like for a camera, and it's in the tongue."

James turned over the shoe to explore its leather tongue. Having chewed off his fingernails, he struggled to pick at the edges. Lexie's nails were shorter than mine, so I stepped up, gently nudging James aside. He didn't like that.

I ran my nail along the seam between the dark leather of the top of the shoe tongue and the lighter, softer underside. It split behind the sound of Velcro tearing loose. I worked to keep the smile off my face for having bested my brother. My nail stabbed inside the crack and worked like a zipper, opening a small gap on the right of the tongue.

Tucked between the two layers was a memory chip. I slipped it out. "Voilà!"

James huffed. Lexie squealed like a mouse. I passed the chip to James, hoping this might ease the competition between us.

"Over here," he said, leading us to one of the steamer's many desktop computers. He needed a caddy to hold the smaller memory device and he went off in search of one, rifling drawers at the other computer stations.

"Do you think they killed him for whatever's on here?" Lexie asked.

"I don't think we'll know until we see it," James said. I knew him well enough to recognize the suspicion in his eyes. The object of his suspicion, Lexie, missed it completely. I saw mistrust and judgment. My brother was testing her.

"Maybe it's just something he wanted to leave behind for us," I said. "Maybe it has nothing to do with anything, but it was important to him. You know?"

"Like a will or something," Lexie said.

Again, James studied her like she was a painting. What was *with* him?

"I suppose," James said.

"Files, stuff like that," she said.

"You know, in case that's what's happening, why don't you give me and Mo a minute?"

I wasn't comfortable with James telling her to take a hike. "James!"

"Just for a minute," he said, his scolding eyes telling me to shut up.

"Sure," I said. "Just for a minute. Why not?"

Lexie handled it so gracefully. "Of course! I totally get that! I'll just . . . be outside." She looked wounded. Sounded brave.

James placed the chip into the caddy and the caddy into the computer and opened the directory.

PASSWORD:
HINT: Wilford Verse Year?

"It's all yours," I said. "James Wilford founded the Wilford Packet Company. Years later that company became our family's shipping company."

"Duh!" James said. "But what year was that, brainchild?"

"No clue. Besides, that's not it," I said. "'Verse.' He's talking about the family Bible. Bible verse. The Wilford family Bible. Remember?" We'd discovered it inside a secret room off Father's office.

"I do," he said. "But the date?"

"Sixteen something," I said. I knew who knew the answer: a boy James couldn't know was here. "Hang on." I texted Sherlock the question, hoping he'd be awake at this hour. (He claimed to need very little sleep, but I didn't believe it.) Only seconds later, my phone's screen lit.

> 1696

"Try 1696," I said. James gave me a look. He knew whom I'd texted, just not what time zone Sherlock was in.

The password worked. James opened the main folder.

The chip's directory contained at least fifty folders. A quick sample of the contents of the various

238

folders revealed more folders, each containing hundreds of files.

I pointed.

MORIARTY

James double-clicked.

I spotted the file first. "Look!" I pointed to a video file. "Check out the date!"

"Father," James whispered.

"The night . . ." I couldn't finish. It was the date of his "accident," a date neither James nor I would ever forget.

James directed the cursor arrow to the file. "Should I?"

"I think so," I said.

"I don't think you should see this, Mo," James said solemnly. "Why don't I look at it first? If it's something . . . you know . . . bad . . . then why should both of us have to live with that?"

I wasn't going to argue. I'd have nightmares for weeks—maybe all my life—if it showed what I thought it might show.

James clicked on the video file. I looked away from the computer but caught eyes with my brother. I saw our life together. Our partnership. I saw, in my mind's eye, the photo of Mother being put into a car. Our homes at Beacon Hill and on Cape Cod. A brief spark connected us. It included the unspoken-of: the Scowerers, Father's accident, Ralph's car crash. Father's secret room filled with treasure. A complicated family history about which we still knew little.

I wanted to look. I wanted this to help reconnect James and me. But I couldn't do it.

James gasped. "It's . . . bad. Real bad." I heard him swallow. "Our security cameras. The foyer."

"Oh, no," I gasped. I didn't have to look. I knew what there was to see.

My brother's voice cracked as he choked out: "Father was murdered."

CHAPTER 46

WITH MY EYES TRAINED ONTO MY SHOES, James messed with the video. He wrote down a bunch of numbers. "The recording starts and stops when there's movement," James explained. "There was a meeting that night. You can look now: I've written down the times so I can stop it from showing the bad stuff."

James and I watched segments of the video several times through. We didn't speak. He'd divided the video into scenes: the arrival of Hildebrandt, Crudgeon, and Lowry; Lois bringing a tray to the downstairs library. Lois leaving the library.

Lois returning with a pot of coffee. Lois walking Hildebrandt to the front door. The two of them talking. Lois returning toward the kitchen. Father leaving the library with Crudgeon and Lowry and showing them out.

James started the segment running again when Lois walked Hildebrandt to the front door. It showed Lois and Hildebrandt talking in the vestibule. Lois passed the camera in the direction of the kitchen. The time—on the bottom right of the screen—advanced twelve minutes. Father escorted Crudgeon and Lowry to the front door. Father headed back toward his study.

James wrote something onto a piece of paper. I was too absorbed with the video to pay much attention.

The clock advanced fifty-seven minutes. Father—not Lois, not Ralph—answered the front door. A red-letter crawl ran across the bottom of the video.

"What's that?" I asked.

"An alert," James said. "I think it's warning of a hack. It's our home security system." He wrote as he continued, "It's not an IP address," James said. "IP addresses don't use colons."

"Speak English," I said.

"Thing is," James said, speaking mostly to

himself, "since when does Father open the door?"

I longed to involve Sherlock. He would know what was going on. I tried to think like him. "One step at a time," I said. "Father goes to the door. He obviously greets someone. The missing video is of whoever that was."

"Duh."

"You don't have to be mean," I said.

James was too busy writing down the security warning. The video continued to run. Suddenly, there was Father lying on the foyer floor next to the stepladder. I looked away so quickly after, I'm not sure I actually saw what I thought I saw. But I would never forget the first time I saw Father's murder.

Not ever.

Apologizing, James stopped the video. I was crying. James hugged me. The way his chest was shaking I think he might have been crying too. "Don't worry, Mo," he said dryly. "I'm going to get whoever did this."

"We are," I said, choking on my tears.

James folded and slipped his scribbling into his front pocket.

"What do we do now?" I asked. "What do we do with this? It's obviously important evidence."

"It was left for me," James proclaimed. "Mr.

Lowry left it for me."

"But I found it!" I said.

"I would have. You know that," James complained.

I felt I had to remind him. "We both lost him, you know?"

"I'll put the video on its own thumb drive," he said. "I'll show it to Colander."

"You promise?" I pressed.

"I promise."

"What about the rest of the stuff?" I asked. "All the documents. Whatever else is on the card?"

"I'll go through it," James said. "At least enough to know if it's important or not. If it is—"

"We both should," I said, correcting him. "Lexie, too."

"No!"

"What's wrong with you? We can divide up the folders. We'll each take a few." Before James could interrupt, I kept talking. "The sooner we know what Mr. Lowry left for us, the better."

James ejected the card from the computer. "Sorry. I can't allow that." I fought him for it, but he held it away and pushed me back. He stuffed it into his pocket with the note. "Mr. Lowry told me about some of the family business. It's private for now."

"Like sending you to military school?" I said.

"Shut up!"

"Promise you won't delete anything."

"Promise. You've got to believe me."

"Why do I have to believe you?" I asked.

He considered my question.

Before he could answer, the door opened. Lexie slipped inside and shut the door.

"Someone's coming!" she said, running toward us.

CHAPTER 47

James and I were used to avoiding getting caught. Having Ralph and Lois around the Boston house had been like having three parents keeping an eye on us. We had to be crafty and sneaky to have any fun. James had an instinct for such surprises. He seemed to know a fraction of a second before I did that we were about to be caught.

Lexie lacked our instincts, but was just plain smart. With the main entrance to the makerspace being near the photo lab, we were out of sight for now, but the open floor plan left us few places to hide.

Lexie pulled out the power plug to the computer faster than it even occurred to me that the light from the monitor would give us away. In the same split second, both James and I fell to our hands and knees, our reaction to a possible bust.

I crawled over to the only box of any size, an empty cardboard shipping box for a printer. I quickly and quietly turned it on its side so I could crawl in, its opening facing the wall.

As I did, I saw Lexie locate a piece of fabric—probably from a weaving project—lie down amid several rolls of other materials, and pull it over herself.

"Who's there?" A low voice. Either a proctor or a member of the expanded campus security team.

What I saw next, just as I was about to stuff myself into the box, astounded me.

James had crawled beneath a lab table. He must have had some kind of plan—James was full of plans—but it had failed. Panicked by the man's voice, he scrambled across the floor, pulled the fabric off Lexie, *dragged her by the ankles into the open area*, and hid beneath the fabric himself. An astonished Lexie got her feet under her and into a crouch.

"You!" the voice thundered as a flashlight beam hit Lexie on her back.

I hid in the box, hearing, not seeing the rest.

"Stand up where I can see you. Turn around! Name?"

"Alexandria Carlisle."

"Dorm?"

"Bricks, Middle Two."

"Your dorm mistress?"

The question, along with the unfamiliar voice, suggested a security guy.

"Ms. McKower."

"It's past curfew. I'm going to call her. You understand?"

"Yeah, I know the drill," Lexie said. So did I. So did James. A curfew violation after midnight meant your dorm master had to stay with you until you were back into bed. It meant a lecture. Demerits. Eventually, a talk with the headmaster and another lecture. Sometimes, a call to your parents. Students could also be suspended or moved into a different dorm.

"Where are the others?"

"What others?" she said. My heart did little flips. Lexie was lying to protect us. Even James the Jerk. "Look. I'm behind on a project. Who knew summer school was going to be so hard? You're going to call Ms. McKower and get me into trouble and that'll mean I have even less time to get this stupid project done. Have you ever tried to three-D print a sphere *inside* a cube?" The guard didn't answer. He was probably still working out what it meant to 3D print something. "I'm supposed to not only know how to write the code for that, but print it and hand it in by third period day after tomorrow."

"You're saying you're working." He made it a statement. "Doing homework?"

"You think I come here to have a good time?"

"What's with that?" he asked.

I couldn't see what was going on, but I sensed it.

"That shoe? No clue. Someone else's project, I guess. It's a makerspace. We make things in here. Maybe someone's making a spy shoe for Double O Seven. You know . . . click your heels it shoots somebody."

The guard chuckled. "You mean like Q."

"Excuse me?"

"Q's the guy who made all the cool stuff for James Bond."

"Yeah, like that. We can make anything in here. But we can't make a curfew violation go away." Lexie sounded like a lawyer working a judge in *Law & Order*. Alone in a cardboard box, I smiled.

"No," the man said, sounding unhappy. "You can't make that."

CHAPTER 48

I LOOKED AT JAMES ONLY ONCE THE FOLLOWING day, a seething, nasty face across the breakfast dining hall letting him know what a jerk he was for what he'd done to Lexie. The rumor mill already had Lexie in the steamer to kiss George Platen, a story fueled by the fact that George Platen tended to follow Lexie around like a sad dog and that he'd left school for home that same morning. The second, and truthful, rumor was that George's grandmother had fallen down some stairs and his parents wanted him home for a few days. But Lexie was being endlessly teased by others making kissy sounds at her as she passed.

When James pulled a no-show at lunch, I briefly hoped he'd done the right thing and gone to the headmaster to explain his having set up Lexie. I could have done the same thing, but Lexie had already made me promise I'd do no such thing. "This is between James and me," she'd said. "You getting in trouble isn't going to change anything."

"But if I get in trouble, then James gets in trouble. And that's pretty sweet."

Lexie had considered what I'd said, but only for a second or two before telling me she wouldn't talk to me for two weeks if I tried such a thing. In summer school, two weeks amounted to an ice age, so I kept my word and my nose out of it.

I didn't have a direct line into James's inner circle of rejects, but I knew Shelly, who knew Tim, who knew Thorndyke. By sports practice that afternoon, I heard that James had left campus suddenly and was due back by dinner.

Apparently Headmaster Crudgeon had personally approved James leaving for Boston. A proctor was visiting the Massachusetts Institute of Technology that afternoon, and agreed to take James and return him in time for study hall.

James was dropped off at the Boston Public Library, but only for show. He walked eleven blocks through sweltering heat to reach the reflecting pool at the center of an old church and a bunch of office buildings.

James took the elevator to three different floors because he couldn't remember which floor he wanted, and Interpol, the international police force, didn't put its name on the building's directory.

He wasn't exactly shown a warm welcome. First of all, he was an unchaperoned kid. Second, he had no identification beyond a school identification card. But he also had Detective Superintendent Colander's business card in his pocket, and that convinced the receptionist to make a call. It was longer than the other calls James had seen her make from the cushioned bench where he waited. A lot of talking and listening, interspersed with suspicious glances in James's direction.

At last, an Asian lady met James and offered him something to drink on their way to the man's office. James requested orange juice. After three other suggestions, he settled for bottled water.

"You may go in." She knocked lightly and pushed open the door. The lady left to fetch his bottled water.

James stood still in the doorway.

"Hello, James. How can I help you?"

"I'm sorry," James said, "I think I have the wrong office." He stared at the plaque on the man's desk.

DETECTIVE SUPERINTENDENT COLANDER

The man's black head was shaved bald. He looked younger than Hildebrandt but older than Crudgeon. He wore wire-rim glasses, a brown suit with a green tie, and an expression of open curiosity.

"I'm looking for the other Detective Colander," James said.

The man smiled widely. "And when you find him, I hope you'll introduce us. I'm from Denmark, James. My father, obviously also a Colander, had one brother, and he was killed in the Afghanistan conflict. He was with the International Red Cross. He's the only other male Colander I've ever met. Other than my father." Another of those smiles. "I'm told you're in possession of one of my business cards. May I see it, please?"

James walked tentatively into the small room, remembering it well. He and I had sat on the chairs currently pushed against the wall. James volunteered the card. It matched a stack of others held in a plastic stand. The man examined it carefully.

"That's mine, all right, though he added a direct number by hand."

"Private number, he said."

"How exactly did you come across it, James? Please, sit!" It was a command.

James sat. "I . . . ah . . . I was here. With . . . I still don't understand: Where is Detective Colander?"

"Now you're worrying me. Are you feeling well?"

"Yeah. Sure. Fine. But . . ."

"I am Detective Colander. This is my office. What exactly are you telling me?"

Embarrassed, James did what Father had instructed him to do: he asked to see the man's official identification. Had he ever done that with the Colander he knew? he wondered. He couldn't remember ever asking. The detective seemed impressed that James would make such a request. He came around the desk and sat next to James. This Colander was a big man. Close up, his eyes loomed large and full of care.

"There's a law, James. A very important law. It's called impersonation of an officer. Are you familiar with what is meant by impersonation? Someone taking the place of a police officer?"

James nodded.

"You understand that if this is a dare or part of some kind of practical joke or—"

"It isn't! I promise you. He isn't you. You aren't him. I came here—"

"Yes?"

"Never mind. I'm so confused."

"Impersonating an Interpol officer results in jail time, James. Do you understand?"

"He said he was you."

"Then you must help me find him. He must be arrested and charged."

"I don't know how to find him," James said. "I mean, the phone number, I guess." James checked his phone's calendar and guessed at a date. "I think he brought me into this office on that date. I have a witness. My sister was with me."

"This office? I was on paternity leave on that day. A baby girl. Our second. My assistant, whom you've just met, would have been here. What time was it?"

James couldn't think. They'd been in the library. Colander had taken them here. Lunch hour? he wondered. He said nothing. It was all too over-whelming.

"You didn't call to set up an appointment with me. Today, I mean." The man suddenly sounded like a detective.

"No."

"Why not?"

"I knew you'd see—he would see me."

The big man nodded. "And you say you're in summer session at Baskerville Academy?"

"Yes." James glanced at his watch and lied. "Oh, gosh. I've got to meet my ride!" He apologized for the visit.

Detective Colander tried but failed to get more out of James.

"If we don't talk now, we're going to end up talking at your school," Colander said. "You don't want that, now, do you, James?"

"I guess not. I don't know. I guess it's okay—"

James, in the midst of a complete meltdown, was trying to figure out who the other man might be, and more importantly, what that man had to do with Father's death. Everything and anything James had told the fake Colander now gained importance. James mumbled another apology for leaving, which he hadn't done yet. Then it occurred to him to stand up and try to leave. Would the man stop him?

Colander called out, practically begging James to stay.

James put one foot in front of the other. He passed the lady carrying his bottle of water. Neither of them said anything to the other. James kept walking.

Impersonating an officer.

Lies.

Murder.

James had been tricked from the very beginning.

CHAPTER 49

RETURNING TO THE MAKERSPACE MADE ME
uneasy, given the last time. Despite having nothing
to worry about, I was on edge. I was there to work
with Ruby Berliner on the photograph of Mother
and Father on the street. Using Ruby's artistic skills
and my knowledge of photography, we turned the
face in the car into an enlarged image on one of the
computers.

At this level of magnification, the old photograph turned into a bunch of dots. It reminded me
of some of the artwork that hung in the hallways of
the art department—weird abstract art that I didn't

understand. But Ruby saw shapes where I only saw the dots. Using an electronic sketch pad and stylus, she added her own at a furious pace. It was almost like a woodpecker pecking at a tree. Her dots joined the others, forming shapes, heightening colors, extending lines. She moved the image right to left and up and down, continuing to peck away on her pad, adding more and more dots.

"How long is this going to take?" I asked.

"Hang on. I'm kinda busy here," Ruby said.

"It's just I don't see exactly what you're doing."

"I'm doing what you asked me to do."

"Right, but what I asked you to do was to try to make the face more real, since it's basically just a blob."

"*Was* a blob," Ruby said. "Let me work here, Moria. Go do something else or get me a tea from the Tuck Shop."

Annoyed with her, I headed over to the Tuck Shop. I wolfed down a Milky Way to settle my nerves. I wasn't a big fan of anxiety eating, but it worked. I got Ruby the tea and headed back over.

There was a worker with a wheelbarrow and a rake off to my right. He was hunched over a bed of flowers doing something or other, when he happened to look in my direction. But he didn't *happen* to look anywhere. He did it on purpose, at least that's what I thought, because it was the same guy from the Vanilla Bean. Talk about a panic moment. I needed another candy bar, and fast.

I stopped so sharply, some of the tea spilled out of the sipping hole in the cup's plastic cap and burned my hand. I also stared right at the guy, and for all I know, my chin was down around my waist somewhere. I'm sure I looked like a complete moron and about as subtle as a duck doing ballet. He looked. I looked. He went back to his flowerbed work. I struggled to force my paralyzed legs to move one foot in front of the other and continue walking as if nothing had happened. But boy, had it happened.

This guy was either spying on me or under orders from James to protect me. Either way he was scaring me.

Making things even weirder, the only person who could clarify this for me was James, and I wasn't about to ask him for anything. I couldn't forgive him for the way he'd sacrificed Lexie. So selfish. So cowardly.

Juggling the tea to open the door to the makerspace, I stole another look in the direction of the gardener. His back was turned toward me; it was as if our little encounter had never happened, as if he was just a gardener and I was just a student. But I knew differently. I knew something strange was going on. It was yet another Sherlock moment, me wishing desperately my friend would appear and have answers to all of my questions and solutions to all of my problems. How many friends did I have like that? I wondered. One. And he was presumably still washing dishes or cutting carrots, or mopping floors at the Vanilla Bean, and I had to pretend he didn't even exist.

Ruby was still at it, hunched forward to the screen, her right hand pecking. She had found a rhythm, comfortable now with the method. She worked with confidence.

I set down the tea.

She grabbed hold of it and spun it to her lips without taking her eyes off the screen, that right hand of hers dropping dots to fill in the space in the enlarged photograph, all of it at such an extreme enlargement that I still had no idea what she was doing.

"So, you ready?" she asked.

"That's funny. I was about to ask you the same thing."

"Don't forget you owe me your dessert tonight and tomorrow night."

"I haven't forgotten."

"And you know we're talking about apple pie and ice cream tonight."

"A promise is a promise."

"Okay," Ruby said, "remember, this is only half the face, so there's more to do."

"No problem."

She made the image smaller and tighter. The orbs took shape: a part of a cheekbone; an earlobe; an eyebrow. All at once, a head appeared, or half a head was more like it. She had been working on the left side of the face, which had been the brighter half in the photo. Where once there had been a vaguely recognizable blur, there was a face. I suppose I must have gasped or coughed or made one of those unexpected noises, because she turned her head violently in my direction.

"You like it?" she asked.

"No . . . I mean, sure, I guess. I mean I like what you did, how you did this. I don't even get how you did this."

"But you don't like it."

"I don't like *him*," I said, my heart somewhere up near my chin.

There was no mistaking the man in the car across the street watching my parents.

A younger Mathias Hildebrandt.

CHAPTER 50

When I returned from the makerspace, Lexie stood just inside my dorm room, pale as ash, her lower lip trembling.

I invited her inside and she sat down on the bed. Her knees shook like Jell-O. People tell you things by the way they move. By the things they do, and don't do.

I asked her what was wrong.

"I need to talk to this policeman. Calendar."

"Colander," I corrected. "He's with Interpol. He's not really a policeman. More like . . . I don't know."

"I need to speak to him."

"O-K," I said. "I thought we were a team."

"We are."

"So why aren't you telling me more?"

Lexie looked at me. Her eyes were glassy. Her lip continued to tremble. She was crying inside.

"It's about James. I need to talk to him about James."

"Hello? I'm his sister! What about me?"

"I can't," Lexie said.

"But . . ." I felt hurt. "Seriously?"

"He's your brother."

"I'm aware," I said. I thought I might stop her lip from moving if I made a joke. It didn't work.

"It's hurtful," she said. "Really, I can't."

"Lexie, now you have to! I'll never stop thinking about it."

She hung her head. Shook it side to side.

"You have to," I said more forcefully. I knew she *didn't* have to. I crossed my fingers.

"I caught him in my dad's office."

"James?"

"After we sailed. Just as he was leaving. He went down to get something he'd forgotten. When I got down there, he was in my father's office."

"He's like that. He explores everything."

"I didn't think anything about it."

"Lexie?"

"My dad was hit by that car three days later."

"What's that supposed to mean?"

"I shouldn't have told you. Please. The detective."

"Colander." I shivered, recalling him showing up at the Bean. "He told me he thinks James is hiding stuff about Lowry."

"And you didn't tell me?" Lexie sounded angry.

"I . . . I guess not."

"Please," she whispered. "I need to text Colander."

"Yeah. OK. I've got his number. But don't accuse James of stuff. Tell him the stuff if you have to, I guess. But this is James we're talking about."

"I know." She nodded. "There must be an explanation."

"There must," I said. But I heard in my own voice how uncertain I was.

CHAPTER 51

"LISTEN, YOU BEING A TECH NERD AND ALL, I need to ask you something," James said to Claudette. He'd stopped her in the hallway between classes. Wearing tight clothes only made her look thinner. Her legs were way longer than James's, but about the thickness of his forearms. Behind her back, other girls claimed she had an eating disorder, though James made it a rule not to believe rumors.

"You don't have to be so charming," she said, deeply sarcastic.

"Sorry."

"No, you're not, which only makes it all the worse. You pay me. I get it. You treat me like you're my boss. I get it."

"I don't mean it like that."

"Of course you do," Claudette said. "How else do you mean it?"

James thought about it. Too long. She snorted.

"Just as I thought," she said. "So, what's the assignment? And I want double what you paid me last time."

"I'll give you a twenty-five percent raise. No more."

"Double or nothing."

He appraised her partial squint, tight lips, and flaring nostrils. "Agreed," he said. He needed this handled.

Her face didn't so much as twitch.

He'd copied the long string of numbers, colons, and letters that had flashed on the Beacon Hill security video. 00:11:B6:C4:99:6A. "Does this mean anything to you? A code, maybe? A serial number? Is there a way to look up that format of numbers?"

"It's a MAC address."

"You mean like an Apple Mac? A computer?"

"Yes, but no. MAC: media access control number," she said, as if James were the stupidest kid in the world. "It's like a serial number, but different. It's like your house has a mailing address. So does your computer. Like that."

James explained the flashing red number he'd seen on the security video. "If it's like a house address, can you look it up?"

"Yeah. I mean I can't look up where it was on a particular night, only where it is now, if that matters," she said.

"I'll take anything." He passed her the paper with the address. "Just do it fast. And as long as we're at it," James said, "are you as good with audio as you are with video?"

"Try me," she said.

"Check your email. I'm going to be sending you some audio files to reassemble. If you do it right, I'll pay you triple."

"You're a real charmer, James."

CHAPTER 52

Surprised by how little money it took to win favor, James continued to spread around some of his cash. That included paying students who constructed the sets for the school plays. James had a little drama of his own planned.

The set designer and the stage crew were already working on the summer play. It had a small cast and three sets. Secretly building another set wouldn't be any trouble, only cost, and James had the money to pay them and buy the supplies. His mission was to create a little magic.

He showed the set designer a bunch of photographs.

"Has to look like this—*exactly* like this."

"This plain? No big deal. I get it. We can do that."

"Seriously—exactly like this," James said.

"I said I got it."

"Two nights from now. And I need the auditorium's blackout curtains in place and some special lighting."

"I can get Tim Wormser for the lights. No problem, I'm telling you."

James promised the kid more money if it all worked out.

A few minutes past lights out, sitting in front of his closet full of computer screens and displays, with Thorndyke looking over his shoulder, James replayed a recording from a hidden video camera inside Hildebrandt's apartment. The man was speaking into the phone. All sorts of things were swirling around James's busy brain: Colander, Hildebrandt, Father's *murder*.

More interesting, he went about his solutions to these complications in a methodical, deliberate way. Criminal solutions, to be sure. Just as his installing the cameras and projectors into Hildebrandt's apartment had been a criminal act. He justified this by thinking that complex problems required complex solutions.

James switched the main screen to a live image inside Hildebrandt's bedroom. The tubby man wore blue pajamas as he climbed into bed. He picked up a bedside book, clearly considered reading it, and set it back down, switching off the lights.

As the room went dark, James switched views to a camera that read heat instead of light—an infrared camera. The furniture was hardly visible, while Hildebrandt's shoulders and head glowed green.

"That's just plain spooky. What's this all about?" Thorndyke asked. He was not the hottest flame in the fire.

"My father . . . It wasn't an accident. They killed him, and I think I know why, and I think I know who."

"Hildebrandt."

"I think so. I can't prove it. Not yet. I have a plan to find out for sure. When I know for sure, that person's gonna pay. You know? That doesn't go unpunished." James's voice was a kind of wolf growl.

"Good luck with that."

"Let me tell you something, Thorny. No matter how old you are, you have fears. Big ones. Small ones. Maybe snakes or spiders. Maybe you're afraid of the dark or a headmaster. Everybody's afraid of something."

"Girls freak me out."

"There you go! You're about to see why I had Claudette put the projectors in Hildebrandt's bedroom. You know Scrooge, and all that? Him seeing ghosts and getting all freaked out?"

"Like the movie."

"It was a book first, Thorny, but yeah, like the movie. Seeing the ghosts." He paused. "Thing is, Hildebrandt drinks a lot of wine at dinner. He drinks after dinner. He's gotta be pretty much blotto by the time he goes to bed. That helps us."

"It does?"

"You'll see."

"I will?"

"Check the hall. Make sure Cantell isn't on patrol." James motioned to the door.

"He did the rounds. He's not coming back."

"I said: check it."

Thorndyke obeyed. A moment later he told James the hall was empty and quiet.

"Then here we go," James said.

"Go where?"

"It's an expression, dough ball. Grab that chair over there. You're going to want to watch this."

CHAPTER 53

"THIS IS LIKE WATCHING *AMERICAN HORROR Story* or something."

"Quiet, Thorny." James was losing patience with his dimwitted friend. His finger hovered over the keyboard, twitching as if it rested on a trigger.

"Having so many views is so cool."

"Thorny! I'm working here."

"Got it! Sorry."

Between the three displays, James had the infrared view of Hildebrandt's dark bedroom, along with two different angles from the tiny security

274

cameras. One looked across the bedroom. Another aimed toward the head of the bed.

The first key he pressed triggered a small speaker Claudette had hidden behind an air grate. The next key played James's voice slowed down to where it sounded like a bear farting. *"M . . . ath . . . i . . . asssss."* James played the odd recording a second and third time. The man's name groaned into the room.

Hildebrandt snorted and sniffled.

"Here we go," James said, pressing another key. He loved this sense of control, like a video game but real life. Big Shot Mathias Hildebrandt in his pajamas, in his bedroom, with James playing the puppeteer. James smiled privately.

On the bedroom wall facing Hildebrandt, a faint image of a man appeared. Faded and foggy, the faceless man swirled like cream poured into a cup of coffee. James tripped the key again. The image vanished. He triggered the sound.

"M . . . ath . . . i . . . asssss."

"The voice of Christmas Past," Thorndyke said.

"If you can't stay quiet, you're out of here," James said.

"Sorry."

"M . . . ath . . . i . . . asssss."

Hildebrandt struggled to sit up. James turned on the projector once more, but only for an instant. He switched it off as Hildebrandt reached for the bedside light. Leaned back. "That's it."

"What-a-ya mean?" Thorndyke exclaimed. "This is just getting good."

"Drunk or not, he's not stupid. Too much and he'll figure it out. Hitting him when he's just waking up or fading out, that's when he's not clear enough to think right."

"But you want him terrified, right?"

"A guy like him? Not likely. I want him . . . bothered, I'd guess you'd say. Upset. Wondering. Off balance. Preoccupied. Like it's the night before exams."

"That's the worst! I never sleep."

James couldn't imagine Brett Thorndyke worrying about exams. "Bad sleep affects everything," James said. "Lois always told me and Mo that. If he's thinking clearly, we'll never beat him. But if we can get under his skin . . ."

"You're mean, you know that?"

James looked over at Thorndyke's hulking frame, his deep-set eyes. Thorndyke could beat the snot out of James with ease, but it wasn't going to happen, because James exerted authority over the guy. He glanced at the screen. Hildebrandt looked around the room, sipped some water, and once again reached for the bedside lamp.

The room went dark.

CHAPTER 54

I SAT ON A LOG, PETTING THE SOFT GREEN MOSS that clung to its bark. Little yellow hairs stuck up from the moss like alien antennae, tickling my palm. The afternoon sunlight caught moisture or dust, or both, in the air, creating streamers of bright, heavenly light like something from a ceiling mural in a church. I was warm but not sweating. My best friend in the world sat next to me, smelling of deep-fat fry oil. Seen in profile in that particular light, he had a sharp and prominent beak of a nose, an exceedingly straight chin, and a long neck.

"Thank you for coming," I said.

"I've told you before, Moria. We're friends. It's what friends do."

I was seriously interested in discussing what he meant by the word "friend." Before I could find the strength, he saved me.

"Did you know tree squirrels fake burying nuts and fruits to fool thieves?" he said. "They exaggerate their burying techniques to throw off birds and other squirrels."

"I did not." He knew I did not. He was merely showing off. Sherlock nearly always started a conversation with the upper hand.

"Native Americans took it as a symbol of trust, preparation, and thriftiness."

"Fascinating," I mocked. "Moss was the first plant on the planet."

"It has no roots, stems, or flowers," he said. "It attaches itself through rhizoids that may look like roots, but they are not."

"Another deception," I said, "like the squirrels."

"You do catch on."

"I try," I said. Sherlock didn't make conversation. If he said something it was for a reason. With him, one either paid attention or was made a fool.

"It's him, isn't it?" I said, indicating the printout of the photograph that included various areas and enlargements of Ruby's enhancement techniques. I'd emailed it to him the night before. "Hildebrandt."

"It would appear so. Yes. What do you want to bet this coincides with your father buying his first train pass?" Sherlock asked.

"Mother didn't run away, didn't leave us," I said, wondering if it could be true.

For years, I'd struggled with her abandoning us. Cried. Gone without sleep. Ached. I was sure James had, too. Her leaving had hurt so deeply I could barely consider that it wasn't true. Why would Father have lied about that? To defend himself? To protect us? To protect *Mother*? I felt off-balance and dizzy. How could half my life be a lie?

"What we know and what we presume to know can end up a kind of braid that when woven together prevents us from seeing the truth of the thing."

"You're saying I shouldn't jump to conclusions."

"I am. Exactly that," Sherlock said.

"Father could have been hiding her. He might not have known Hildebrandt was looking on."

"One of ten or twenty possibilities."

"Am I being paranoid?"

"You're wounded. Did you know—?"

"Not again!"

"—that wounded animals will run miles with the herd, never showing their condition? They say it's shock. Adrenaline. I'm guessing it's more like the animal doesn't even know it has been wounded, or, even if it's hurt, it still has something to prove."

"If you have something to say, just say it, Lock."

"Very well. Your father removed your mother from your house for her safety and protection. There's no evidence of applied force in the photo. It looks cooperative on your mother's part. Hildebrandt either had something to do with causing the move, or at least had knowledge of it. We'll never know if your father or Ralph was aware of the man spying from the vehicle across the street."

"Never say never."

"That is, your father isn't going to tell us," he said, showing no concern for my feelings whatsoever. "Nor Ralph." Lock passed me a Boston transit map. He'd drawn a circle in yellow highlighter. It stopped where it reached water.

"Far as I can tell," Sherlock said, "judging by the cost of his credit card charge for the rail passes, he could have traveled anywhere inside the circle."

"So, all of Boston. Big help, Lock."

"An understandable, if incorrect reaction, Moria."

"Incorrect, how?"

"Isn't there some expression for missing the little thing because of the bigger one?"

"I'm sure. There's an expression for everything, Lock. We call them clichés."

"Focus, Moria."

"I'm missing something."

"You are," Sherlock said.

I studied the map. "OK. I get it. Sorry. It's not about what's inside the circle, it's about what's outside of it, which isn't much."

"Go on."

"You said before that you buy a ticket by zones. The zones represent distance traveled. Father bought the farthest zone. So, like I said, it's not that he *could* travel anywhere in Boston, it's that he could only ride as far *outside* of Boston as your yellow circle."

"I do enjoy your company."

I bit back a smile. "It's large. The circle is huge. We can't search several hundred towns and villages for my mother. If she's even alive. . . ."

"No," he said.

"Why do you do this?" I asked.

"Do what?"

"Don't give me that! You tease me. Test me, and my patience."

"A thing isn't truly learned if it's told. It has to be discovered."

"So, you're my teacher? Ick!" I recoiled.

"And you, mine."

"Really?"

"No. But I thought you'd like hearing that," Sherlock said.

"I detest you!"

"False."

"Double detest for you saying that."

"Double false." He tapped the map in my lap. "Use your resources, your brain, your memory. Eyes open, Moria! You and James told me a story. A train ride? A town?"

"Do you know how many times James and I have been on trains? In towns? Was it in Europe or the United States?"

"Now who's the snob?" asked the British snob.

"United States, I'm thinking. Boston, I'm thinking." Tired of his condescending expression, I lowered my eyes to the map.

"Oh Godfrey!" I shouted, seeing the name of a town—Manchester-by-the-Sea—just inside the yellow ring he'd drawn. "James and I followed Father there."

"So you told me."

"There was another guy."

"Yes. Now think, Moria: What organization did that other man belong to? Probably?"

I squinted my eyes shut. I remembered the beach. Gadwall Specialist Center, the huge institution up on a bluff. We'd lost track of Father inside that place. An awful place, I thought, my memories flooding back.

"Who might have been keeping an eye on your father? Not to spy on him—as you and James thought—but to protect him?"

"Oh, come on!" I grabbed his arm.

"That'a girl," he said.

I could have punched him.

CHAPTER 55

Shutting off the alarm clock, James felt
fresh and excited despite the 4:00 a.m. glowing on
the clock. Day two of James's plan.

James put in his earbuds and switched on the
screens in the closet.

Hildebrandt slept, a green blob of warmth on a
black screen. James understood his plan was risky,
maybe stupid. But the stagehand on his payroll had
let him know the special set would be ready, and
that a change in rehearsal schedule limited James's
use of the auditorium to just two nights.

He had to risk it.

James projected a piece of a home movie. It wasn't clear who'd shot it. Ralph, maybe. It was one of those Mom-and-Dad-play-with-the-kids to show how normal the family is. Father had his Big Bad Wolf going, his face locked into this toothy growl, wide-open eyes, and stretched frown. To a six- or seven-year-old it was terrifying. Caught on grainy film, he looked mental. Like something from a horror movie where the guy creeps out of the dark basement and sneaks up on the woman doing the dishes with her back turned. Father the psycho killer.

"*M . . . ath . . . i . . . asssss.*" Then again, slightly louder, as James caused the video to repeat: Father's face unseen, then turning quickly and looking right into the lens. Spooky.

"*M . . . ath . . . i . . . asssss.*"

Hildebrandt seemed to levitate off the bed. He looked like a kitty cat in the cartoons where all the hair sticks out. He seemed to lift off the mattress and land before screaming as he tried to sit up. His elbow gave way, dumping his face into the pillow.

James shut off the projection, but kept recording.

Hildebrandt spit out a series of bad words. Angry words. He screamed. "I'll tear your throat out! Squish you like a bug!"

James couldn't have written it better than that.

He had it recorded! All he needed now was to get the file to Claudette. Along with the other recordings he'd already provided, he hoped that would do it.

Two birds with one stone, he thought, pushing his chair back and crossing his hands over his head in a brief and long overdue sense of victory.

CHAPTER 56

BEING TAKEN BY THE ARM UNEXPECTEDLY AND
hurled into the Main House might have made
another girl scream. Not me. I had James for an
older brother. His form of communication often
involved a push or a shove, a tug on my hair, a
clamp on my arm.

We ended up in the World Literature classroom.
The two of us, a few minutes before dinner. James
knew the route I took between the dorms and the
common room. I was a victim of my own routine.
Stupid me.

Not wanting to give him any sense of control

over me, I pretended as if this were the most ordinary way to meet up with my brother.

"What is it? I'm hungry."

"You're always hungry."

"My staggering brain power requires nutrition," I said.

"He's a fake. Colander's a fake."

I shuddered inside as James recounted his visit to Boston that resulted in the discovery of the lie. I thought I might faint. Superintendent Detective Colander of Interpol, the man who had detained my brother and me, the man who seemed to pop up like a whack-a-mole, the man who'd interrogated me in the Vanilla Bean only days before asking for my help with my brother. This brother. The boy sitting in front of me. Had James gone off his rocker as the detective had implied? Who was I to believe? More importantly, whom to trust?

Having no control over my breathing meant I didn't speak.

"I have a plan," James said. "It's complicated. Dangerous, I suppose. Risky, to be sure. I need you. He'll be less suspicious of you. Way more less suspicious. And there's this. A peace offering."

James dug into his pocket and produced the leather string holding Sherlock's master key.

I reached for the leather necklace. It was there,

where it belonged. "I don't understand," I grunted.

"Without this," he said. "Mo, this key changed everything. *Everything*. I know where Hildebrandt lives. I've been watching him."

I pulled the key out of my shirt to show it to him. As I did, I remembered him handing it to me in the pool after it had torn off. "You switched it," I said, my heart clenched. "You *stole* it from me without even asking!"

"I'm sorry."

"You're *sorry*?" I needed CPR.

"There's so much to tell you."

I nodded angrily. "I'm listening!"

"I think it could be Colander who Father let into the house. A detective, right? He'd have to let him in, I think. If he did, that means Colander killed Father."

I slumped into one of the classroom's rolling chairs.

"At least," James said, "I think it's possible. I can't prove anything. Not yet. That's why I need you."

Lexie! I thought. I'd sent a group text for her and Colander to meet. "Me? I need the truth, James. What were you doing in Lexie's father's office?" It just came out. I knew that look. I knew my brother. *Guilt!* "Oh, James." My eyes sprouted tears. My chest felt clawed open.

"Did Lexie tell you that? She and Hildebrandt . . ."

I couldn't hear this. I covered my ears. I heard it anyway, muffled and like from another person. "I know she talks to Hildebrandt, and she lies about it."

I shook my head violently.

"Why would she do that? I have proof, Mo." He found the notepaper rubbing in his back pocket. It was smudged, but I saw the outline of numbers and letters. Familiar numbers and letters. "I took that from Hildebrandt's place. That's Lexie's number."

"So what? That's your evidence?"

"Why does he have Lexie's number?"

That was it. That was all I could handle. It was more than I could handle. Each of them calling the other the traitor. Only one sane voice in all of it, a voice I remembered from a café closet. Was Colander a fake? Had he killed our father?

"James: we both know Lexie. You're messed up. Both of you are. But you didn't kill her father, and Lexie isn't a spy."

"Of course I didn't kill her father!"

"But?" I said. I could hear it hanging between us. James was thinking back to Espiranzo's claim:

"We don't kill people." Was it true? "But . . . you can't ask me how I know this. I don't actually *know* it."

"But?"

"It's possible . . . just possible Hildebrandt did."

"We need Sherlock."

"News alert: he's in England. Besides, it would take forever to explain everything even if we could find him."

"You just don't like him."

"He's strange."

"He's brilliant."

"He's in England."

"No. He's here, James. He works at the Vanilla Bean."

My brother and I entered a staring contest. He knew I wasn't lying.

"If you don't shut your mouth," I said, "you're going to catch flies in there."

CHAPTER 57

LEXIE'S MEETING WITH COLANDER WAS PLANNED for late afternoon. I hurried to her dorm to head her off. Gone, her roommate told me.

In hopes she was somewhere on campus, I tried the Tuck Shop lounge, the common room, the mail room, and Main House.

It turned out a good thing that none of the students obeyed the academy's cell phone rule. We all owned phones, we all carried them. The rule simply meant you didn't use it in public, and you kept it silenced. Out of sight was out of mind. Only stupid use resulted in your phone being confiscated. My phone's Find My Friends app put Lexie in the academy's indoor tennis facility, a quarter mile from the varsity soccer field and the northernmost building on school property.

I texted James. Knowing he sometimes ignored texts, I left immediately for the tennis facility. James would have to catch up.

He did—riding shotgun in a groundskeeper golf cart being driven by the same peculiar man who'd been watching me at the Vanilla Bean.

"Meet Espiranzo," James said, introducing me to the cart's driver. "He knew Father. We can trust him."

Espiranzo said nothing. The cart bumped along, drove down from the far end of the soccer field, and raced for the pale brown metal tennis facility with its domed blue metal roof. The cart jerked to a stop by a side door.

"Open the door quietly. You will not be seen. Stand still and wait for me."

James climbed out. I thanked Espiranzo for the ride.

"You are welcome, Moria," the man said, displaying what to me was an uncomfortable familiarity. He reached back for a black plastic case on the seat behind. "I'll join you in a minute. James knows what to do." His swarthy face offered an ominous look. He had something bad planned. That black case was part of his plan.

James carefully eased the door shut behind us. Voices—two voices, Lexie's and a man's—echoed faintly off the metal walls.

The facility housed six tennis courts wrapped in sections of a thick dark green plastic tarpaulin hung as a curtain to catch balls. James and I huddled. Besides serving as a backstop, the tarpaulin created a walkway so players could move court to court without disturbing play.

James motioned me forward with him. We walked silently and oh so slowly, because our body movement threatened to cause waves in the plastic walls and announce us.

"The thing is," Lexie was saying, "at the time, I don't know, it all seemed so normal. Not that any boy had asked to come to my house before. I don't mean like that."

James glanced back at me. Stunned to be hearing Lexie saying this, he also had a message of innocence intended for me. He was literally caught between the two of us. I looked away. I couldn't stand to see my brother so stressed. His expression of innocence might have convinced others, but not his sister.

I saw Espiranzo's back, creeping down the

narrow corridor in the opposite direction. I wondered why. I wondered if I'd mistaken James's looking at me. Had he been looking past me at Espiranzo? Was that look on his face the result of something he and Espiranzo had planned?

I made a face to show James my confusion.

He pumped his open palm. It said, *Calm down*.

Calm down? My stomach felt like a Vitamix.

Colander spoke too softly to be understood, or maybe my ears were ringing.

"I'm not trying to get James in trouble," Lexie said. "I don't mean it like that, but—"

"It's fine. Have you two had a fight?" Colander asked. He said something like that. The distance and the steady whine in my ears didn't help anything. In truth, the tennis facility was so cavernous, sound didn't travel clearly. He could have been saying something about the "night," or "light," or "blue" instead of "two." I wondered if I was inventing most of what I heard. Imagination can be a blessing and curse.

Lexie sounded like she was upset.

We were closing in on them.

I looked behind. Espiranzo had disappeared. That didn't help me calm down.

James dared to peek out between two of the large curtains. He motioned up, suggesting Lexie and Colander were somehow above us. A viewing deck, I realized, as James led me to the end of the corridor, through a door, and upstairs. Our eyes reached floor level a few steps from the top. I saw Lexie's flip-flops and Colander's scuffed oxfords. I eked my head higher: their knees and waists and the edge of a table. Higher still, the back of Colander's head, Lexie's in partial profile. Her eyes darted. She saw us.

Colander watched her expression change. He was turning his head as James spoke.

"Stop, Lexie! He's a fake."

Colander stood. James and I surfaced.

"He's not who he says he is. Has nothing to do with Interpol. He killed Father."

Colander smirked. Lexie went pale. The air turned electric. I could see dust particles floating like spaceships. I could hear James's breathing. Struggled to find my own.

"The guilty will say anything, Alexandria," Colander said. "James is a desperate boy. What do you think, Alexandria? James the Innocent, or James the Member of a Secret Sect?"

"Think about it, Lexie!" James said. "How could he know that?"

"Because I'm a superintendent detective of an international police force, James. Do you really think lying is going to help your case any?"

"I met Superintendent Detective Colander, and he isn't you. You aren't him."

"It's true, Lexie," I said, speaking for the first time. I had no idea if it was or wasn't, only that I was trusting my brother more than this strange man. "James went to Boston to Interpol. This guy isn't Superintendent Colander."

"That's interesting, Moria. Because I have identification," Colander said. He reached into his suit coat. I expected a gun. He passed a thin wallet to Lexie.

"A forgery," James said. "He's a fake."

"You've got it all figured out, don't you, James?" Colander sounded like one of those teachers who thinks he knows everything. At that moment, I knew he was lying. It didn't necessarily mean James was telling the truth, but I believed James.

James's serve. "Mr. Lowry left me video. Don't worry, I've made several copies. What you didn't know was that Father hated heights." I nodded, supporting my brother. "He would have never climbed that ladder. You faked his accident. You faked how he died."

Lexie stepped away from Colander.

"You live in a fantasy world, James. Lexie just explained you were invol—"

"It's true, Lexie! I looked at your father's calendar. But that's all I did. Anything else . . . that wasn't me. But given how tight you are with Hildebrandt, you must already know that."

"Me? I have never, ever spoken to that man. I never met that man," Lexie said.

I knew it was the truth. James knew it was the truth.

Colander broke the silence. "The three of you are in big trouble. You will need to get yourselves lawyers. You will have to come with me."

Again, the man reached into his suit coat.

"No, they will not." Espiranzo stood at the top of the stairs behind Colander.

I heard a pop.

Colander's suitcoat opened, revealing a gun.

I tackled James, rolled, and knocked Lexie's legs out from under her. I had no idea how I'd done that.

Colander never touched his weapon.

He slouched, spun halfway around, and spilled off the chair.

A dart with a fuzzy blue tip stuck out of his back.

CHAPTER 58

I MAY HAVE FAINTED. I'M NOT EXACTLY SURE.
Colander's eyes remained partially open, his body
still. Espiranzo had killed him. By association, I
was an accomplice. I was going to jail for murder.

That's when I saw the fallen man's chest moving.

"He's alive," I said.

"Of course he's alive! We must move him
quickly," said Espiranzo, slipping the dart gun
into his belt. "Help me get him on my back,"
he instructed my brother. As the two dealt with
Colander, I'm not sure if Lexie or I ever moved.
Espiranzo bore the man on his back in a fireman

carry. He descended the stairs. "I'm going to need you to get the door."

"I'm sorry I looked at your father's calendar, Lexie," James said. "I don't know if it had anything to do with . . . but whatever . . . I should never have done it."

"You used me. You'll go to jail."

"I don't understand how Hildebrandt had your phone number, but he did."

"I have never spoken to him."

"I saw it on a notepad. I've been watching him. He made a call. Your line went to voicemail at the same time."

She said something she shouldn't have. Roughly translated, it said James was the same as the business end of a horse.

Obviously, I couldn't hear James thinking. But if I'd been able to it would have gone something like: "If she's telling the truth, and I think she is, then how did Hildebrandt get her number? Why would he have wanted her number? Moria wouldn't have given it. I didn't. So . . . ?" He spoke for real. "The video," he said. "Hildebrandt . . . and . . . oh, Helena, Montana. Lois spoke to him when he was leaving our house that night. Remember the two of them at the door?"

"Lois?" I said. "What are you saying? Our Lois?"

"When I got the gold—"

"You what?" I said.

"Lois knew about the gold. Don't you see?"

"See?" I said. "I have no idea what you're talking about."

Espiranzo called for someone to get the door.

We all took off at once.

CHAPTER 59

THERE WE WERE IN HARD AUDITORIUM, LEXIE, James, Claudette, and I. Espiranzo, too. Despite it being night outside, the tall windows were covered in thick blackout material. A cube—a room— occupied the stage. Bland inside, with gray walls and a single light fixture. Colander sat in a chair, his hands tied tightly to a ring on a table bolted to the floor. James and Espiranzo moved the final wall into place, at which point the only view on the inside was over three flat-panel screens set up on a collapsible table, where Claudette was already working with video and audio equipment.

"What is this?" Lexie whispered into my ear. James had warned us not to talk, not to say a word.

I shrugged, having no idea what James was up to, or how he'd arranged all this. His mention of Father's gold came to mind. I was not in the best of moods.

With the final wall in place, Espiranzo entered the room through the door. Lexie and I watched it all on one of the three flat-panel screens. The groundskeeper stuck Colander with a hypodermic and gave him a shot. Espiranzo left the room.

Five minutes passed. Maybe ten. Colander coughed and came awake. He sipped from a straw in the plastic water bottle left for him.

"You have . . . disappointed me." It was not a voice I knew. I startled. I hate to say it, but I was comforted when I realized Claudette was doing something at the computer to play the man's voice. Listening carefully, I could tell the words had been patched together, but even the way the voice rose and fell made it sound so realistic. The groggy Colander wouldn't hear us.

"Moriarty," the voice said.

"That's Hildebrandt," Lexie whispered.

"I thought you'd never spoken to him," I whispered back.

"I haven't," she said.

James shot us a look. We shut up.

"We had a deal," Colander said, like a man only half awake. He spilled some water trying for another drink. "Where am I?"

I knew how to recognize when my brother relaxed. I had the feeling he'd expected Colander to know this room. The fact that the man didn't seemed to help my brother.

"Moriarty," Hildebrandt's recorded voice said. It sounded slightly different than the last time. "These are dangerous times for us all."

Lexie nudged me, cupped my ear, her words warm. "I'll bet that's from some speech he gave. Cut and paste. You see?" I didn't see a thing, except James's silhouette and, on the monitor, Colander tied to the table. "Claudette's using his speeches and stuff to make up whatever she wants him to say. When James is pointing to the table like that, I think he's showing her what line to play. It's like the movies!"

"*Mission Improbable*," I said.

"You. Moriarty. Why?" Hildebrandt said. James had to be counting on Colander being zonked from the dart. Stringing words together like that made them sound slightly awkward. Who spoke in one-word comments?

"You know why," Colander said. He sounded

more cautious, more careful. Threatening. I wondered if the drug was wearing off.

There was too long of a pause. I could see something was wrong. Claudette worked the keyboard furiously. On the screen, Colander looked around at the room all the more carefully. "Where am I?"

"Tell me," Hildebrandt's voice said.

"Why be such a coward? Show yourself." Colander craned his neck to look into a large mirror on the wall. He tried for the water again. This time he could be heard sniffing before he took a sip. "I know you're on the other side. Come in here if you want to talk to me."

"Tell me," Hildebrandt repeated.

"You tell me: What day is it? What time is it?"

James appeared to panic. Colander was testing him. James pointed down at the list between him and Claudette.

"Go ahead." Hildebrandt's voice. Pause. "Moriarty." Pause. "Tell me. Or. I'll tear your throat out. Squish you like a bug."

"I should have known better," Colander said, "than to trust you. 'Common interest,' you said. 'Serves us both equally.' Bulldog. That's all I can say!"

"We have a problem," Hildebrandt's voice said.

"Maybe you do. My problem is your problem

now. You have failed to keep your word. Hands off, you said. Yet, here I am."

"Moriarty."

Colander huffed. "Day and time." He sat back. "Do whatever you're going to do."

A red flashlight beam signaled from behind us. Its presence meant one thing: *trouble coming.*

It all happened so quickly. Espiranzo appeared onstage, a gun or the tranquilizing gun in hand, aimed at the side wall of the stage set. James or Claudette, or maybe both, hitting switches that shut down the screens and stage lights. The auditorium went pitch black. All but the light that seeped out at the edges of the constructed box onstage.

A voice from behind us said, "Don't shoot. Gag him!" Espiranzo moved.

Lexie tugged me to the floor, my head dizzy. Didn't I know that voice? We lay down flat between the rows of seats.

A narrowly focused sterile-white penlight beam appeared on the floor of the aisle I faced. It moved quickly toward the stage. All I glimpsed was a pair of shoes and pants. Strange, given my reaction. I might as well have been bitten by a snake. My blood ran hot, frying my brain. Emotion surged through me chemically, a brightly burning ball racing through hollow limbs. It settled into my stomach.

I wanted to throw up, to be rid of it. I wanted it out of my chest. Out of my body. If it stayed inside it would tear me apart. I had to scream or cry or shout or stand up or kick. I lacked all control. The venom filled me.

I knew those shoes.

CHAPTER 60

"HIDE. NOW!"

I knew that voice.

I stood. James stood. We were both noticeably shaking.

Ralph, our old driver, our protector, a man who was supposed to be dead, whose funeral I'd attended, shined the flashlight onto me, and then James. "I will explain to you both. I promise. For now, there's no time. Hide backstage. Not here. All of you! Hurry!"

Maybe it was because I was so stunned to see a man who'd died in a car wreck. Maybe it was the years of conditioning—Ralph was always telling me and James what to do, and we obeyed him like he was our father. Maybe it was love and relief and joy. I told Lexie to get up. James and Claudette hurried onto the stage. I ran into the aisle, wanting to hug Ralph, but he moved away, toward the auditorium doors. As Lexie and I climbed the short steps to the stage we could hear Ralph speaking beyond the auditorium doors.

The next muffled voice belonged to Crudgeon, and, after that, Mrs. Furman.

James burst from the backstage darkness, running past where I hid toward the front of the auditorium. Lexie grabbed my arm, preventing me from joining him. She and Claudette pulled me past a second line of curtains to where props and large pieces of sets were stacked. We crawled into one.

Lexie wrapped her arms around me, probably less to do with comforting me and more like self-preservation on her part.

I was sobbing.

CHAPTER 61

JAMES PLACED HIMSELF WITH HIS BACK TO THE wall alongside the auditorium's two sets of double doors. A matter of a few yards to his left were the stairs leading to the balcony, one option for a quick escape should the grown-ups enter.

"You would rather not enter," James heard Ralph say.

"You've already said that, and I told you to step aside." Crudgeon.

"What you don't see and what you don't hear about, cannot be held against you in a court of law, Headmaster. I beg you to reconsider."

"You're saying laws are being broken. This is my school!"

Ralph asked respectfully that Mrs. Furman be dismissed. The headmaster did as Ralph asked. James stood there trying to make sense of Ralph being able to boss around Headmaster Crudgeon and what that might mean in terms of Ralph's rank in the Scowerers. It also caused James to realize Crudgeon had apparently not been surprised to see Ralph, a man James had presumed—no, confirmed—dead.

Ralph spoke quietly. "The individual inside is extremely likely the head of a certain European organization whose interests run counter to our own."

"You brought such a man here?" Crudgeon said irritably.

"I did not, Headmaster."

"Oh, I see. You mean . . .?"

"Yes."

"Extraordinary."

"Yes."

"Here? Why?"

"I will find out for us," Ralph said. "It appears . . . that is, they needed the stage. They've replicated a room. A place. I can't be certain. That's how it looks."

"They?"

"Yes."

"Extraordinary," Crudgeon repeated, sounding in awe. "Replicated?"

"Honestly, it looks like something they probably saw in a film. Television, maybe. But they've done quite a thorough job of it. I don't think you want to know more than that: some students misusing the stage for some kind of prank. Plausible deniability. If Mr. Lowry were alive we could ask him. But then again, my sense of things is that his death may be what has brought us to this point. James is a dog with some bite, Headmaster."

James shuddered with the compliment.

"And so he should be."

"Yes," said Ralph.

"Impressive."

"It is."

"I should leave."

"I think it best for all. Best for the society." Ralph meant the Scowerers. He knew Crudgeon would do whatever was necessary to protect the Scowerers.

"You'll brief me," Crudgeon said.

"In your capacity as headmaster? Only if necessary. For now, you can tell Mrs. Furman that some students were using the auditorium to rehearse and that I convinced you to look the other way. That overachievement was not a punishable offense."

Again, James was struck how Ralph spoke with

such authority to Headmaster Crudgeon.

"Very well," Crudgeon said.

"How was it you were informed?" Ralph asked.

"I was told there was a Pargo missing," he said, referring to the campus golf carts. "That security had found it parked behind the auditorium. I thought some students were taking joy rides. Nothing much to do about it. But up close, security saw some light coming from the auditorium. That suggested the blackout curtains, and that I wanted to see for myself."

"A member of the faculty intervened," Ralph said.

"You? Faculty? God help us."

Ralph pushed open the door, walked past James without seeing him.

"You let me believe I'd killed you," James said in a choked whisper. He'd slid down the wall, propped on his haunches.

Ralph turned. He also spoke softly, to keep the man in the room on stage from hearing. "A cruel and horrible thing for me to do. I suspect you'll never forgive me. All I can say is that it had nothing to do with protecting me, and everything to do with protecting you and Moria. I don't expect you to believe that, even after I explain, but it's true. Sadly, now's not the time. I told you to hide, and I meant it, James. You're not to witness what comes next. Certainly not Moria. Not any of you. You're to get them all back to their dorms. School protocol will require the headmaster to order a room check. This all has to go into the books properly to protect the society. It means Espiranzo and I must act very quickly to make use of the good work you've done."

"I outrank you," James said, testing. He wasn't sure of this.

"Indeed. It's true. You're the governor. The final choice is yours, if that's how you want it."

"That's how I want it," James said strongly.

"And I'm glad to hear it."

"I'll do it your way," James said.

"Glad to hear that as well."

"I will monitor it. Alone. I won't record anything. Are you going to hurt him?"

"We're going to establish a dialogue, you might say."

"You won't kill him. Not here."

"Of course not. Not our way. That's for them, the Meirleach. Not our way unless it can't be helped."

"Colander's one of them," James said.

"Aye. He's one of the Meirleach's command. It took you to ferret him out. Well done."

"You're sure of that?"

"I will be, in about twenty minutes," Ralph

said, sounding sad and disappointed. "This isn't a part of the job any man should enjoy."

"No."

"Why this?" Ralph pointed to the stage.

"It's a room in Hildebrandt's basement. I doubt Colander's ever been there, but in case he knew about it . . ."

"A wise choice." James could see Ralph was thinking. He waited for the man to speak. "That will require a different tack. Pay no attention to my lies, James. They are a means to an end, that is all. If they sound convincing then I'm doing my job correctly. Understood?"

"Yeah."

Ralph put his hand onto James's shoulder. "This is a side of me I'd rather you didn't see."

"I have to know about Father," James said.

"And so you shall. But I will need something from you."

"Okay?" James sounded tentative.

"Your phone, and a quick lesson on how to use it."

CHAPTER 62

"You?" Colander's ghostly expression was understandable. James had felt the same way upon seeing Ralph upright and breathing. Watching the monitor and listening in on headphones, James felt a world away instead of a matter of yards. He'd made me and Claudette wait backstage, from where we only heard parts of conversations. We strained, each gathering different bits.

"Me."

"Where am I?"

"At the end of the line," Ralph said.

"You working for Hildebrandt? I don't believe it," Colander said.

"I could say the same thing." Ralph allowed the man to believe he'd betrayed Father. "Did you really think we—he—would make an alliance with our chief rival?"

"You and the woman, Lois Agnew? You *both* were his agents?"

Lois? I nearly screamed! Suddenly her conversation with Hildebrandt on the video, the night of Father's "accident," made sense. My drinking a hot chocolate that had put me to sleep and nearly drowned me months before.

"Who do you think kept tabs on Moriarty for him?" Ralph played to the one-way glass as if addressing Hildebrandt on the other side. James understood immediately that it wasn't Ralph's first interrogation. "He needed someone inside. Who would he choose?"

"You? What you suggest is not possible."

"Because Lois was your contact? Lois, who let you into the house once the video had been compromised." Ralph paused, clearly hoping Colander might confess. Nothing. "Lois, who arranged the robbery and took a bruised face to keep suspicion off herself? You think I didn't know about that?"

Colander shook his head. "Not possible."

"Do you think Mr. Hildebrandt would rely upon a single source, a single spy? He ran the FBI, Colander. You think he's stupid?" Ralph looked at the mirrored window again, making Colander think Hildebrandt was watching. Listening. "He used you to do the dirty work. To take out Moriarty. But you betrayed him."

"Not true!"

"The Meirleach meeting with Moria Moriarty off campus? That was not part of the agreement."

"Unplanned, I assure you."

"Mr. Hildebrandt would like to know the meaning of that meeting. All that was said."

"A coincidence seeing her there. Nothing more."

"You have been playing the role of a detective, Colander. How many detectives believe in coincidence?"

"It was nothing."

"To you, perhaps. To us, you went too far. You violated the agreement. Do you know what happens when one violates such an agreement?"

He swore. "I kept my part of the agreement!"

James held his breath. I held my breath. Ralph had zeroed in on our father's "accident."

"Do I need to remind you of that agreement?"

Colander spoke to the mirrored glass, imagining Hildebrandt on the other side. "You wanted Moriarty gone. We wanted him gone. 'Common interests,' you said. This is—" Another swear word. "I didn't question your motives. I carried out my part of the agreement!"

Colander had just confessed to the killing.

Colander hollered at the glass. "Come out from behind there and face me yourself! You're a coward!"

Ralph slapped him across the face, as any employee of Hildebrandt's would. "Respect, my friend. Tell us about the girl. Why the meeting with the girl?"

"I . . . she was . . . It's her brother. The attorney Lowry. There's evidence against"—Colander pointed at the mirror—"you! All of you. I warned the girl to tell her brother to stop. That's all. A warning."

"When the Scowerers hear it was you who killed Moriarty, where do you suppose that will leave you?"

Colander didn't like the question. He also didn't contradict Ralph's accusation. "We have an agreement."

"You have no proof."

"Mr. Hildebrandt promised we would block the security video for you?" Ralph chuckled to himself. "That's what he told you, wasn't it?"

Colander looked concerned and tense.

"He played you. You must have expected that such a thing was possible."

"Nice try." He sounded arrogant as he explained to the window. "We *both* recorded our agreement. Have you forgot—?"

A sneeze echoed through the auditorium. Colander sat up, alarmed not only by the sneeze but the sound of it. Both were wrong for a small interrogation room in Hildebrandt's basement.

"Oh, but you're a clever one!" Colander said. "Where are we? You tricked me! A warehouse, is it? Sounds like one! OK! I'm done talking. Kill me if you like."

"You both recorded the agreement," Ralph said, improvising. "How stupid are you? He's a hero to every cop in the country. Your recording will go missing before it can ever be heard in court."

Colander was no longer so arrogant.

"You will be dropped somewhere. Without injury. Without violence. I'd run fast and hard if I were you. It won't be Mr. Hildebrandt after you. It will be your own people!"

Colander sat stone-faced and silent, staring down at his tied hands.

"You should have left the area," Ralph said. "Personally, I don't understand why you're still

around, but I can guess: greed. You. Hildebrandt.
Everyone is after Mr. Moriarty's fortune. Let me
tell you something. I worked for him for years. I
have no idea if it exists or where it might be. Personally, I think it's a myth."

Ralph waited several more minutes for Colander to explain himself.

Then Ralph walked out and left him for Espiranzo to handle.

CHAPTER 63

"This can't be," James said, despite my having told him.

But in fact it was Sherlock who sat down with Ralph, Lexie, and me at the Vanilla Bean's corner table. James looked like he'd seen a chicken wearing a tuxedo.

"Key," Sherlock said, abbreviating my brother's middle name, Keynes.

"Lock," said James. "How in the world—?"

"You're just lucky, I guess." Sherlock gawked at Ralph. "He is risen."

"Will miracles never cease?" said Ralph.

Lexie and I took in these exchanges like an audience at a play.

James filled the silence. "Superintendent Colander, who is a fake," directed to Sherlock, "gave up Hildebrandt as the mastermind behind Father's 'accident.'"

"Not exactly," Ralph corrected. "More like implicated. We've no real evidence. And in the battle of he-said, he-said, Hildebrandt will come out the winner ten times out of ten."

"So, we're planning an intervention," said Lexie. "James and I followed real evidence—blood—back to—"

"The observatory," said Sherlock. "Yes, I know."

Light flashed in James's eye. "That was you in the woods!"

"It was," said Sherlock. "Backup, you might call it. Woods can be dangerous at night."

"You scared the spit out of us!" Lexie said.

"Speak for yourself," said James, as if he hadn't been frightened. To Sherlock: "We've been punking Hildebrandt at night. The man likes to drink and we've made sure he's had nightmares. Mostly visions of my father. Video on the wall. Voices. Three nights now. He's more freaked each night. It's working. We have one last surprise for him."

"A visit from me," Ralph said. "The spectral me. The ghost of me. I've seen the video James has, and it's quite frightening. Very well done. Only the headmaster and Mrs. Furman now know I'm alive. Not Hildebrandt. We must act quickly though! Colander will run. When he does, word will spread quickly. Power plays for control of the Meirleach will be set into motion. If we're to trick Hildebrandt, it must be now." He addressed Lexie, "Sorry if much of this is not making sense. We have no time to explain it fully."

"No problem," Lexie said. "How can you trick a man like that, anyway?"

"I will tell you how, but only the once. Should you ever repeat it, I will deny it." He looked into the eyes of each of us. We nodded one by one. "Something you, James, and Moria don't know: I was a Boston policeman as a young man." My heart sped up. Ralph had more secrets. "I did something bad. I took money to remove a piece of evidence from our evidence room. It helped your father, eventually, because it involved the Hildebrandt family. 'What goes around, comes around.'"

"The pistol in Mr. Moriarty's office desk," Sherlock said dryly. "Correct me if I'm wrong, but that weapon was involved in a robbery of an armored car in the 1960s. James, Moria, and I found a newspaper article concerning that robbery."

"Hildebrandt has an article framed on his wall," James added. "It says it's what got him started in law enforcement."

"Ironic, it should say that. You children are enterprising young lads. And lasses," Ralph said, including me and Lexie. "You've pieced this all together, have you?"

"Not until this moment," Sherlock said. "The real story has been elusive."

"The real story goes back a long time. A rich father protecting his son. A wet-behind-the-ears copper who made a mistake that nearly got him killed."

"But you kept hold of the weapon, didn't you?" Sherlock sounded about thirty years old. "You gave it to Mr. Moriarty for safekeeping. Shrewd, Ralph. Very shrewd."

For the past week, I had been working so hard on Mother's final photograph that much of the conversation didn't interest me. But this last part, about Hildebrandt's manipulation of Colander, jumped out and startled me into focus.

"And Mother," I said, drawing the attention of all at the table. I explained the photo, Ruby's brilliant computer work, and the discovery. Upon hearing my explanation, Ralph did not look comfortable.

"I left you that photo at the Cape house, Miss Moria. And the note in the darkroom before that."

"I was watching over you. Helping you along where I could. Mr. Lowry had entrusted me with the location of the thumb drive. But you, James, had the man's shoe, and I worried what you might do with that information if left to yourself."

"You," I muttered, my head reeling.

"Moria, you were at the Cape house with Lois. That was dangerous. It was time you and James knew about your mother. I'd found that picture in your father's things. I hoped you might be clever enough to work out who it was across the street."

"Hildebrandt," I said. "It's him watching from his car. Across the street. Ralph, you were there. Did you see him? You were there."

"I was driving. Yes," Ralph said, though it carried a tinge of uncomfortable confession. My naming Hildebrandt had affected him. "Never saw that car until the picture. Didn't know Hildebrandt was there until right now."

"Mother did not leave us," I told James.

"Mo, we've told each other that for the past six years."

"Remember Father's trip to Gadwall?" I said.

James's eyes flared.

"We never knew who he was visiting?" I said.

Ralph appeared deeply troubled. "How could you know that, Moria?"

"I didn't," I said. "Not for absolute certain. Not until just now. Thank you, Ralph!"

James was crying, though trying not to. "Mother's alive."

"I hope so," I said, my eyes searching Ralph's.

"Your mother's alive."

"Astonishing," said Sherlock.

CHAPTER 64

James, Ralph, and I made the drive to Boston in silence. It was like old times except no one was laughing. Ralph wouldn't tell us what he needed us for but it had to be something important to go to all this trouble. Maybe he just didn't want us arguing with him. Or maybe he still didn't have a real plan.

I couldn't stop looking at him. Grinning. I'd never met anyone who'd come back from the dead. He seemed something of a miracle to me.

To Lois, too, apparently. She screamed as he came in through the back door of our Beacon Hill home. James and I heard her because we entered through the front door at the exact same moment. We were on a mission to recover a key from the ashes, and a gun from a secret drawer.

Ralph provided us cover.

CHAPTER 65

SHERLOCK DIDN'T SHOW UP.

Ralph, Lexie, James, and I waited impatiently in the Baskerville woods, but no Sherlock. James, who'd moved his monitoring equipment from the auditorium into one of the three backstage dressing rooms, called Claudette. He called the room "Command Central," which struck me as childish, but then again, I was a mature twelve-year-old girl.

"He's still not here. I hate to leave the girls alone," James said.

"We are happy to be alone," Lexie said, interrupting the call. I seconded her remark.

"How hard is it to keep a lookout, Sherlock or no Sherlock?" I said, struggling to believe my own words. Sherlock was a fast thinker, a clever boy unlike any I'd met. "I'll take the back and the observatory. Lexie, the front and opposite side. You said yourself, there's only one bodyguard at night. We've got this."

"He patrols the property." Ralph, who carried a rucksack over one shoulder, handed us both small cans of pepper spray to hold off any of Hildebrandt's bodyguards. "In case it comes to that," he said.

"Enough!" I said. I didn't want to consider that possibility. "Any more what-ifs or maybes and I'm going to lose my nerve. Let's get on with it."

"We get on with it when Claudette says to," explained James. "Only then."

We waited. I didn't know if it had been five minutes or fifteen, but suddenly all our phones vibrated at once. I glanced down and read the group text.

Looking around one more time, as if hoping to spot Sherlock's late arrival, James whispered, "Let's go."

He and Ralph took off up the path in the direction of the observatory. Lexie and I followed after a count of thirty. Nearing the top of the hill, we moved through the woods to our right, away from the observatory. Approaching the back of the decaying ruin, I hunkered down where I had a decent view as Lexie continued around the structure and out of sight. She took up position with a view of the driveway. In the palm of my hand, I held my phone, waiting for the go-ahead text. The real pressure was on James and Ralph and we all knew it.

"Good luck," I whispered, far too late for them to hear me. Maybe I was talking to myself.

Lexie texted the group:

> guard in car in front

That was the signal James needed. He and Ralph would head through the observatory and into the tunnel. It was also time for Claudette to project the ghostly images of Father on the walls of Hildebrandt's bedroom.

Ralph paused at the open door to the basement room that so perfectly matched the set built onstage for Colander. He marveled at the effort and determination of the young James to avenge Father's murder. James's planning and the trickery impressed him. James was indeed the choice to lead the Scowerers. The boy was a natural leader born with a sneaky way about him. He'd make a fine criminal mastermind someday.

Up the basement stairs. Down the hallway. Quietly up more stairs to the bedroom door. James paused, hearing his own recorded voice muted on the other side. Claudette was right on schedule. James motioned to the door. It was Ralph's moment.

> **GUARD OUT OF CAR. TWO GUARDS!**

James received Lexie's text too late to stop Ralph, who'd put his own phone away.

> man in back of house

I sent my own text as quickly as I could. He was a tall, shadowy man who gave me chills just watching him walk. I couldn't see him clearly. I wasn't sure I wanted to.

Ralph slipped through the door as Hildebrandt faced the opposite wall, where a flickering image of Father loomed larger than life.

"You can't outrun your mistakes," Ralph said.

Hildebrandt turned around so fast his pajamas barely moved.

"You?" Hildebrandt clutched his chest in pain.

"Was my job to protect him," Ralph said, pointing at the wall.

Nearly a mile away, in a smelly room backstage, Claudette played a simple recording of James's slowed-down ghost voice, recorded a day earlier. "Thank you, Ralph."

The exchange between two apparent ghosts sent Hildebrandt reeling.

"Impossible," he moaned.

It was impossible, but Hildebrandt was too sleepy or drunk, or medicated, to believe it.

A moment later, Father's image flickered and faded. Claudette had shut down the projection of Father as planned. It was up to Ralph now.

From my post, I witnessed that the event changed everything. Ruined everything. It had apparently not occurred to James or Claudette—certainly not to me—how the projections inside Hildebrandt's room would look from the outside. A blueish pulsing and light played on two upstairs windows.

The guard on patrol stopped and looked up. I saw him touch his ear. I could hear him speaking, though not what he said. He headed for the back door. The Old Man was awake, I could imagine him thinking. Maybe part of the job was to check in on him.

back guard into house

front guard into house

GET OUT OF THERE!

The speed with which things happened next could only be explained by Einstein. Time either expanded or compressed, but whichever it was, more stuff happened in one minute than normally happens in fifteen.

"One of your many mistakes," Ralph told the reeling Hildebrandt, "was hanging on too tightly to the past." He looked like a man both drunk and crazy. Not out of his mind, but in an alternate reality. One in which he couldn't find his balance, physically and mentally. Claudette's audio/video work had terrified the man, filling him with adrenaline.

Ralph held up a police evidence bag with a yellowed label. Inside was the gun from Father's secret drawer. James and I had sneaked it out of Father's desk while Ralph had spoken to Lois only two hours earlier.

"I should know. I'm the young cop your father

paid to steal it from the evidence room." Ralph let that sink in. Hildebrandt struggled to make sense of what he was hearing. "A young cop in line with the Scowerers, I might add. I left it for safekeeping with Mr. Moriarty in case something unfortunate happened to me. Funny what young, stupid kids will do. You steal a candy bar just once, and pretty soon you have it in your heads to knock off an armored truck."

Hildebrandt couldn't get a word out, his eyes glued to the gun in the evidence bag.

"This was what prevented you from forcing him or threatening him to go along with your new plan for the society."

Owl-eyed, Hildebrandt looked on the edge of having a heart attack.

"The robbery on the Cape was a long time ago. Those things follow you. You college kids doing such a stupid thing. A guard shot dead. The stolen money never being found."

Hildebrandt went pale.

"The thing is," Ralph said, "when a secret comes apart, it's like a plate being dropped on the floor. Too many pieces to repair."

"Chain of custody will never hold." Hildebrandt tried to sound convinced.

"Maybe. Maybe not. But it can't hurt to have

the confession of the cop who took it. Are you willing to play those odds?"

Knowing Claudette was recording all of this, Ralph considered his words carefully.

"No court will hear it."

"A man is little more than his reputation. Court or not, a story like this getting out will ruin yours. Small satisfaction for you killing Mr. Moriarty, but it may have to do."

"I did not kill Moriarty."

"You arranged it."

"So say you," Hildebrandt said. There was not a hint of intoxication in his voice. It had left when the gun had come out.

"Colander failed you. He took care of Mr. Moriarty, but failed to find the gun, so you cut a deal for him and his Meirleach thugs to return to the house looking for it and the Moriarty treasure. An elaborate plan, breaking in to three different homes."

Just then came a loud noise from the hallway.

James squatted at the top of the stairs as one of the guards climbed steadily toward the second floor in no particular hurry.

As the man reached the top landing, James jumped out and pushed him down the stairs.

The second guard, the one who'd waited in the car, must have been a trained gymnast the way he leaped over his tumbling partner. He used the hand-rail to propel himself up and over and removed his gun as he continued higher.

James did what any idiot fourteen-year-old boy would do: he dove at the man.

Only nothing happened. Or, at least, nothing James expected. He found himself flying back-ward, not down the stairs. Ralph had yanked him out of the way. Ralph had stepped in front of him. There was a yellow flash. A gunshot.

Hildebrandt came out of the bedroom in his pajamas, looking like a wild-eyed madman. James, who'd thumped his head on the floor, found his legs wouldn't move. There was no gun in Hilde-brandt's hands.

Driving to the Cape house a few years earlier, we'd passed a car crash, a minivan on its side. We'd seen a woman—a mother, I think—her face scratched, wandering away from the wreck, wan-dering right into the traffic. Hildebrandt moved like that. Lost. Blind.

James finally felt his legs tingling. He scooched on his bottom in order to see down the stairs as

Hildebrandt climbed over Ralph and the others. Moving like he didn't know he was stepping on people. Hildebrandt reached the front door.

That was when Ralph, who lay atop the two others, attempted to roll onto his side.

He was bleeding.

Badly.

There was no mistaking the gunshot.

I texted Lexie:

stay!

She texted:

OMG

My thumbs were already typing as her next text arrived.

H in car!

The gunshot had made my hearing insanely sensitive. I heard not only my own frantic breathing, but car wheels grinding the pebbled driveway.

Headlights swept the woods and I saw Lexie hiding. She was squatting at the side of a tree. As the light went past her she didn't move an inch.

The engine groaned louder and yet faded as it headed up the drive toward the paved county road.

I texted:

There were probably a hundred things I could have asked, I could have written. I had no idea why I'd sent that exact message. Maybe my fingers and my mind operated from two different areas of my brain. Maybe my heart and brain were so disconnected that my emotions and body operated on different tracks. Or maybe I had a kind of paranormal intuition like one of those birds or butterflies who can fly two thousand miles back to the exact same tree.

Because Lexie texted back immediately:

No

"The Boston apartment," Hildebrandt said from the backseat.

His driver kept driving. His men knew not to speak unless spoken to, not to strike up a conversation. Hildebrandt leaned back.

"Things went from bad to worse," he said.

The driver kept quiet.

"He was real." As if that made any sense. "Gunfire. Somebody . . . On the stairs. I haven't got any idea . . . wait a second! Pull over a moment!"

The car kept moving.

"I said: pull over!" Hildebrandt yanked on the door handle. Nothing. Dove across the backseat to the other door. Nothing. The window. Nothing. "I said—"

"Shut up and listen to me!"

Maybe it was the accent, maybe the driver's confidence, but Hildebrandt strung together a bunch of words that would have gotten him sent to the headmaster's office.

The car slowed, though barely. The driver turned slightly into profile. "Allow me to introduce myself. I'm called Sherlock Holmes."

CHAPTER 66

"**I**'M NOT A GOOD DRIVER," SHERLOCK SAID. "Sorry, your real driver couldn't make it. I don't recommend messing with me when my hands are on the wheel." He sped up the car. The woods streamed by on either side of the road. Even a small jerk of the wheel would result in a head-on crash.

Hildebrandt frantically reached for his seatbelt and clicked himself in. "You are going to regret this, boy. Unless you pull over this instant and turn the keys over to me, you'll face kidnapping charges. You'll go to prison for the rest of your life."

Sherlock tugged the wheel to the right. The car tires yipped. He corrected the wheel only a yard before leaving the road. "Might I recommend you don't limit your kidnapper's options before you have the upper hand? If you give me the choice of life in prison or a tree, I might just take the latter, you know? How would that be?"

Another bad word. "What . . . do . . . you . . . want?"

"It's a long list. Do you have a pen?"

"Do I look like I have a pen?"

Sherlock checked him out in the rearview mirror. Adrenaline had gotten Hildebrandt this far, but he was holding his head like someone who had a horrible headache. His pajama top was torn, a mass of steel wool escaping from his chest. His blotchy face reminded Sherlock of someone about to throw up.

"If you vomit in this car, I'm going to go a lot faster. Just FYI. That's not good for either of us."

"Put the phone down. You'll kill us both."

"You'll speak when I ask questions," Sherlock said, yanking the wheel dangerously one-handedly. "And only then. *Capisce?*"

"You are in so deep!"

Sherlock sped up considerably. "A simple yes or no will suffice. *Capisce?*"

"Yes," Hildebrandt said between clenched teeth.

Sherlock slowed the massive SUV. He'd scared even himself with the last move. He lifted his phone and glanced at it quickly, well aware of the rule not to text and drive. He figured life-and-death circumstances could allow for interpretation of the rules. But he was wrong.

A deer jumped out from the woods. Sherlock overreacted, pulling too hard on the wheel. The car rocked. Hildebrandt let out another example of potty mouth. The SUV caught only the deer's tail as the back wheels of the car lost contact and entered a skid. Sherlock reacted instantly, spinning the wheel the wrong direction. Instead of straightening, the vehicle began a slow counterclockwise rotation like the hands of a giant clock. It would have continued to skid, continued to rotate—right off the road—had Sherlock's magnificent brain not calculated his mistake. He corrected the wheel, turning *into* the direction of the skidding back wheels. The car shuddered, the tires barked, and the grille drifted into the right lane before rocking once more. It was headed in the correct lane, going in the opposite direction as if nothing had ever happened. The deer's twitching white tail and hind end could be seen vanishing into the woods.

"Piece of cake," Sherlock said.

He wasn't sure Hildebrandt heard him. By the look of him, the man might have passed out.

The two guards awoke to a weeping James awkwardly cradling Ralph's head and shoulders. Seeing the man's blood on the stair treads, determining their boss was nowhere to be found, they fled out the front door. A car was heard racing away from the property.

"Look at you, babbling like a baby," Ralph coughed out wetly. "What in the world, boy?" Ralph examined the gunshot wound to his upper chest. "Dial nine-one-one on my phone, will you, boy? And then get out of here. But find me a washcloth first, will ya? I need some compression on it."

"I'm not leaving."

"Of course you are. It's a bleeder, is all. Now help me call an ambulance. You're leaving before you have to answer a bunch of questions you can't answer."

"James?" Lexie's voice from the direction of the front door. She spoke his name louder.

"In here!"

"Go away! Don't touch anything!" Ralph

shouted. "Either of you! Fingerprints. Get out of this house. Now!"

James accepted Ralph's phone and dialed. Ralph snatched it.

"There's been a shooting. Ambulance needed . . . Yes, I'm the victim. Address? Use my phone's GPS. Hurry." He ended the call. He whispered, "It's done. Now go!"

James continued holding the man. "I can't leave you."

"If you don't, I'll give you a good shellacking!"

James smiled faintly. "Good luck trying."

"Go."

"James?" Lexie was coming up the stairs with a dry washcloth.

"You must learn to protect those around you, son. Miss Moria and Lexie will be involved if you don't act."

James looked at Lexie. "For them, then," he said.

"You're going to do fine in your new position, son. Don't try to force it. It will come to you."

"Don't talk like I'm not going to see you again."

"I may be taking an unexpected vacation but I'll stay in touch this time. No visiting me in the hospital if it comes to that. Use your head, not your heart."

James's and Lexie's phones vibrated at the same instant.

"Go," Ralph said.

"You're on a fool's errand, boy," Hildebrandt said. "Sherlock Holmes to the rescue? Is that the plan? Turn me in to the police? For what? You know who I am, I trust. Who's going to believe some high school Brit over the former director of the FBI?"

"You and Colander. Ralph has all the evidence we need," Sherlock said.

"You're just a boy. I'd rather spare you these details. But it appears I cannot. So, you'd better listen, and listen well. If you doubt me, boy, it's on you. If anything untoward should happen to me, *including* my arrest, Moria Moriarty will experience an unfortunate accident. The arrangement was made because of the Moriarty boy, James, not the likes of you, but it's in place, nonetheless. You go through with this, you will set in motion a plan that cannot be undone. Do you understand?"

Sherlock slowed the car.

"Hers will not be a survivable accident. Do we understand one another? This is not a twisted ankle, young man. Your act, and your act alone will account for whatever happens to her. You will have to live with that. I'm afraid she will not."

Sherlock stopped the car.

It took Hildebrandt a moment to realize they'd returned to the entrance to his own driveway. Three figures approached the side of the car from the back, while in Sherlock's rearview mirror, distant treetops flashed with the blue light of a police car or ambulance.

James, Lexie, and I stepped up to the front passenger window as Hildebrandt again struggled to open the child-locked backseat doors. Sherlock rolled down only the passenger window.

"I see you got my text. Good! Get in," Sherlock said. "Climb through the window." The light in the trees grew wider and brighter. "And hurry it up!"

James scrambled through. I approached next.

"No!" Sherlock said. "Only James." He started the electronic window up.

I saw the lights coming quickly toward us. My fingers hooked over the edge of the rising window, I tried to slow its ascent. "Come on, Lock! We're part of this!"

Sherlock looked directly at me. He wasn't known

as a cheery boy, more like thoughtfully quiet. But he wasn't sullen or sad either. Not gloomy or moody. Just *different*. Our connection was intense, his look deeply sorrowful. It was as if he were carrying the weight of the world. Seeing him behind the wheel I immediately understood that he'd anticipated the worst: that Hildebrandt would get free of James's and Ralph's plan and that he would run away. Sherlock couldn't have predicted that both guards would abandon the car, yet I knew he'd somehow known to get behind the wheel regardless. Lock didn't miss much, which is why his look sickened me: he was afraid.

Just before my fingers were broken by the window closing, I yanked them out and pounded on the glass.

"Sherlock!! OPEN THE DOOR!!"

The car sped away.

My heart sank. I felt faint. Sherlock had chosen sides. He'd burned me.

James looked over the front seat into the back. "You're going to pay for this."

"You are very much out of your league, young man. If you have any sense at all—which I'm beginning to doubt—you and your English butler will return me to my residence. This car is GPS tracked. By now my team is in pursuit. Good luck with that."

"You killed my father."

"I did not."

"Mr. Carlisle?"

"I cannot speak freely in front of your . . . driver, but you are mistaken. Again."

"It's a trap," Sherlock said, anticipating James dismissing him. "If I pull over his goons will catch up. He's trying to buy time."

"Drive," James said to Sherlock. To Hildebrandt: "You can talk or not. It's up to you. I trust Sherlock." James turned around and faced front. "You killed my father because of the direction you wanted to take our society. Or, actually, you arranged for Colander to do it for you, which is about as cowardly as it gets."

"You'd be smart to turn around, boy."

"Not going to happen," James said.

"It's kidnapping."

"It's murder."

"Your father, as brilliant as he was, turned a blind eye because of heritage. Legacy. History. He clung to the past. You know this, don't you? You saw it too."

"Shut up."

"He didn't approve of any new thinking. If anything, he was a man who wished for the 'old days' more than tomorrow."

"Why were you there the night my mother left?" James barked. "Across the street in the car."

Hildebrandt required time to recover from the question. "Did your mother leave? She most certainly did. But only because your father was protecting her. It was his idea, James. His solution."

"That's not true."

"Fine. It's not true. You know what else isn't true? Had your father been more flexible he'd be alive today. Knowing our society, do you think it was me, James? Me alone? You're too smart for that."

"Don't try to compliment me," James complained. "You know who's smarter than both of us? The kid behind the wheel. My friend who's driving."

Sherlock didn't deny it. Instead he told their captive, "For an FBI agent, you miss a lot. James bugged your apartment. He has video—and audio—of you. That's called evidence."

"You disagreed with Father about the Eastern European problem." It was not a total guess. It had come up at the meeting of the Directory. "It's why you felt you had to win the vote for Kennedy Wilkes to be our attorney. Wilkes is one of yours, isn't she? You already own her." James didn't make it a question. "But there was Father in your way. Let Colander take out an enemy and let his ignorant son—me—take his place and you'll be able to use your power to get what you want."

"It's money laundering," Sherlock blurted out, as if he knew. "What else do the Eastern Europeans prize more than American dollars? They want cash. That was the proposal, wasn't it? Start doing business with your so-called European partners? Launder their drug money. Their gambling money. All their dirty money."

"Father would never agree to do business with anyone selling drugs."

"Dreadfully narrow-sighted of him," Hildebrandt said. "You, I would think better of, James."

"I told you: no flattery."

"You wanted the truth," Hildebrandt said. "You tell me. Truth or we wait out the ride, providing my men don't catch up to us. I'm afraid it's bad news for the both of you if that happens. They won't be kind, you know? They don't care how old or young you are, only that you took the man it's their jobs to protect. They'll gladly kill anyone who comes between them and me."

"Truth," James said.

"Yes, I proposed to sell American dollars to overseas criminals and, more importantly, the terrorist organizations they represent. Yes, your father objected. For such a brilliant man, he oddly missed the bigger picture. Mr. Holmes, since you're so brilliant, do you care to speculate?"

"No one but a lunatic would do business with terrorists," Sherlock said. "It doesn't require much speculation."

"You see? No imagination. What was my prior job, young man?"

"FBI director," James answered.

"Correct. And, in that role, how often do you think I had to deal with terrorism?"

"Weekly? Daily?"

"Hourly," Hildebrandt answered. "All hours of the day. Every day. Why did I resign? And what did I do immediately after?"

James answered. "I don't know why, but you joined the Directory."

"If you can't beat 'em, join 'em," Sherlock said.

"Something like that. Yes. Sure: make a little money for all those years I wouldn't take a single bribe, not so much as a free dinner. True. But it goes much deeper than that. Much!"

"Terrorism," James said. "But if you care about

fighting terrorism, why leave the FBI?"

"Cheese-Its!" Sherlock cried out. "That is devilish," he said, looking into the rearview mirror. "Did you explain it to Mr. Moriarty, or was he supposed to figure it out on his own?"

"I explained everything," Hildebrandt said.

James badly wanted to ask what it was they were talking about, but didn't want to appear stupid. So he listened.

"He refused on principle," Sherlock said, speculating. "No business with terrorists."

"He was a principled man," Hildebrandt said.

Sherlock eased his phone toward James, who saw the phone was recording. James set his phone to record as well.

"It's bril," said the Brit. He was playing to Hildebrandt's ego. "If you, the Scowerers, played hard to get, but eventually agreed to launder their money, some of those funds would come from terrorists. With a little cyber spying, one could then trace the funds back to the terrorists themselves."

"You see," Hildebrandt said. "A silver lining."

"'Follow the money,'" Sherlock said. "You'd be able to tell your former fellows in government who and where the terrorists were and how they were being funded."

"And, with each effort, make this world a little

safer," said Hildebrandt. "Bravo, Mr. Holmes. Please tell your friend here that it's all I want. A few votes within the Directory, a good attorney to protect the organization, and with some careful work we end the funding of terrorists. We do the things that our government can't do. There are laws, you know. We do what's *necessary*."

The idea hit James blindingly. "The Scowerers act like a bank. We exchange dollars like those booths in the airport. We trick them, follow the money back to who's trying to exchange, and expose the terrorists."

"All that's required," Hildebrandt said, "is to think bigger. Is it illegal? Most certainly. But that's never stopped the Scowerers. Is it wrong to launder drug money? Arms dealers? Terrorists? It is, and it's awful in so many ways. But if it means we catch the terrorists? One man, a single man, a great man, stood in the way of that. His loss is great, James. There is no denying that. One does what one must do for the greater good."

James hurt so deeply, felt so confused, he considered jumping out of the moving car.

Headlights behind them.

Sherlock pushed down the accelerator.

James released the door handle.

"Don't do anything stupid!" Hildebrandt said,

once again clipping into his seatbelt, something both boys had done from the start of the drive.

"Call them off!" James said.

"Do I look like I have a phone?"

Sherlock drove faster. Hildebrandt put both hands down firmly onto the seat and leaned back, eyes wide.

I should have figured that Lexie would know how to drive an ATV. It was like a motorcycle with four wheels. It was as if she knew she'd find one in the storage shed that sat under an elm tree at the end of the gravel parking area. She threw the shed door open and came out riding the thing and shouting for me to climb on.

I told her, like it or not, I wasn't leaving Ralph.

As we were arguing, a black SUV with tinted windows whizzed by. This area of Connecticut being farms and orchards, I couldn't imagine there being another car like that for many, many miles.

"Hildebrandt," I said.

"But they took off going the other way," Lexie countered.

"I hate Sherlock!" I blurted it out. Sadly, it was all I could think about.

Another car flew past, heading in the same direction as the SUV. Hildebrandt's goons. "I gotta go," she said.

"And do what exactly?" I implored.

"Something is better than nothing," Lexie said. "Sure you won't come?"

I nodded.

She zoomed away, headlights off, the rear tires throwing pebbles.

"What do you think?" James asked Sherlock.

Sherlock made eye contact with Hildebrandt in the rearview mirror. He heard my name echo inside the car. Inside his head. "Terrorism, the environment, and nuclear bombs are the three biggest threats to democracy," Sherlock said, sounding like TV news reporter. "As much as I don't want to say it . . ." He looked over at James. "I believe him."

James sat still.

"It's up to you now," Sherlock said. "I don't pretend to know the right choice. But . . . whatever your choice, do not overlook the power you have at this moment."

Hildebrandt did not like the sound of this. He sat forward.

"Your mother," Sherlock said. "This man must be made to pay for what he's done to your father. To your family. His idea can continue to live. That is up to you."

"We know she's at Gadwall," James said, stunning Hildebrandt yet again. It felt good to James to finally know something Sherlock Holmes did not.

"Interesting," Sherlock said.

A fast-driving car, headlights off, pulled alongside the SUV before Sherlock saw it.

"Cripes!" Sherlock said.

A gunshot. James ducked. Sherlock lost control of the wheel. "Tires!" Sherlock yelled as the car skidded off the pavement and into a thin band of dirt and weeds between the road and forest. The SUV plowed over a speed limit sign and a mile marker. They scraped the bottom of the car so loudly it sounded as if the car were coming apart. Sherlock slammed on the brakes. Too hard. The back of the car swerved and hit a tree. The SUV spun around sharply, now facing backward. It skidded to a stop in a cloud of dust. The other car stopped forty feet past them. Its white reverse lights blasted out of the dark.

The SUV's headlights were shining back in the direction from which they'd come. Through the dust, Sherlock imagined he saw an ATV, realizing he must have hit his head, must be seeing things.

Then he saw Lexie behind the handlebars. He released both his and James's seatbelt. Reached across James, pushed open the door and James with it. Sherlock followed outside.

Hildebrandt's guards were running toward the SUV.

Sherlock dragged James toward the slowing ATV. They climbed on with Lexie.

"Stop!" a guard shouted.

Lexie tipped the ATV onto two wheels as she gunned it in the opposite direction. Sherlock lost his balance and was going off the vehicle as James caught him by the arm and hauled him back onto the seat.

"Thank you," Sherlock said. "Invigorating, don't you think?"

"Shut up!" said James, reaching tentatively around Lexie's waist to hold on.

CHAPTER 67

COLANDER, A DANE WHOSE REAL NAME TURNED out to be Magnus As, was arrested for, among other crimes, Father's murder, in what the news called, "a sweep of organized crime." The US State Department claimed it was the biggest arrest of foreign nationals involved in a single criminal organization since a drug cartel had been shut down in the 1990s.

A former director of the FBI being implicated in an armed robbery decades earlier made it into newspapers around the world. No one seemed to know if charges would result from the evidence supplied, but the damage was done: Hildebrandt's reputation was tarnished for good.

Three weeks had passed since the night of all the insanity. I hadn't seen or heard from Sherlock since.

Then, one morning I found myself sitting across from him in our Beacon Hill home's downstairs library. Lois was tied up and gagged and locked in Father's secret room. Technically, the legal firm responsible for James and me had fired her. We intended to go beyond technicalities. It had been Sherlock's idea, of course, but I wasn't giving him any credit.

Sherlock looked paler and thinner than a few weeks earlier. His hair was a scruffy mess as always, lending me the impression he cut it himself with a pair of elementary school scissors. I tried to feel sorry for him. Sadly, I felt nothing at all.

"I'm not sorry we let Hildebrandt go," he said. "There was no sense in turning him over to the police. The way Ralph has handled it was the only way."

"Ralph was in an ambulance! You think that was well-played? You kept me from getting into the car. You left me and Lexie there. That's unforgivable. I don't get why you're here," I said.

"Ralph and James offered for me to go with you," he said.

"That's a stupid idea."

"If you want me to leave, I shall," Sherlock said, in his Sherlockian way.

"Don't do that. Don't put it on me!"

"It is on you. I want to be with you, with you all. It's your call. I will honor your decision."

Darn him! Hearts weren't meant to hurt like mine did. It felt dangerous, destructive to feel your chest clamped in agony.

He rubbed his spindly hands together, trapped between his knobby knees. I fought off a lump in my throat.

"You've got to stop making arm slings part of your wardrobe," I told Ralph as he drove. The rented van remained a bit slower than other traffic. Lois had been moaning into her gag for an hour. We didn't need to be stopped by police.

We passed a sign for Manchester-by-the-Sea. I felt suddenly sick to my stomach.

"Window," I pleaded.

The one-handed Ralph rolled his window down.

He could have killed us! The sea air smelled sweet. I thought of a different James and me. The one where our best friend was the other person, the keeper of our secrets, the accomplice to our crimes. We used to have adventures together. I couldn't read James anymore. Personally, I felt like two different girls: then and now. I thought back to Father, Mr. Lowry, Mr. Carlisle, Colander, Hildebrandt. Nightmare heaped upon nightmare.

I'd been having a recurring dream of standing in front of a mirror, wearing a mask. Each time I took off the mask, another lay beneath it. No matter how fast I removed them I couldn't reach my real face. I was having issues.

When the truck rolled slowly onto and across quiet gravel, my heart leaped in my chest. I didn't look out a window—there weren't any in the back of the fish truck.

But I could see the sign we'd just passed as clearly as if I'd had a window.

GADWALL SPECIALIST CENTER

James and I had once been so close to the truth here. I had to wonder what might have happened if we'd found it back then.

CHAPTER 68

I WOULDN'T HAVE WANTED TO GET ON RALPH'S bad side: he'd thought of everything. The fish truck. Our matching brown carpenter coveralls, so I'd look like daddy's little helper when standing next to him. He even wore a baseball cap that read: Hippo Movers. No idea where he'd picked that up.

He didn't wear his sling, as it might have looked a little suspicious for a moving man to have his arm in one. But his theory—Sherlock's, if I'm going to be honest; the entire plan was Sherlock's, though I couldn't bring myself to admit that—was that institutions like the Gadwall Specialist Center had "guests" (substitute "patients") coming and going a lot of the time (substitute "dying," "being hospitalized elsewhere," "moving in"). A visitor might be questioned. A relative, like me, might be questioned. But no one would take a second look at a moving man, even one with his adorable (let's face it) daughter by his side.

No one did take a look, not even as Ralph accessed a basement loading dock where he'd parked the fish truck. He opened the garage-like door to the outdoors. He and I rode the freight elevator.

Using James's memory of the day he and I had searched the Gadwall Specialist Center, along with Sherlock's uncanny ability to work with numbers, Ralph and I were on the second floor looking for three particular room numbers: 219, 224, and 231.

The first, 219, revealed an older man, balding, with buck teeth and cloudy eyes. Ralph apologized and shut the door. On the way to the next, I stole a look outside at the late-afternoon sunshine and the shoreline that attracted tourists and locals alike. There had been a time I would have been on such a beach, probably at the Cape house. I might have had a floaty, or swim fins and a snorkel, or I might have been bronzing on a towel while the sound of dogs barking in the distance lulled me to sleep. I had a sickening feeling those times were gone for good. I didn't know how that was possible, but the idea of spending my life in jail came to mind.

"You with me?" Ralph, a few steps down the hall. Me, still at the window.

"I'm with you," I said.

A nurse smiled at us as she passed.

Ralph knocked and opened the door to room 224.

I knew her immediately. The photographs. The home movies. She was painting a watercolor that sat on a wooden easel angled toward the window. She was thin. Too thin. She wore a smart blue shirt beneath a paint-stained apron, jeans too big for her, and stained tennis shoes. The room was okay if you liked institutions. Her well-kept hair held gray streaks that reminded me of icicles. Her eyes, gray-blue and telling, didn't change at all as she saw me. But a very small smile took to her lips, and I knew then that she recognized me.

"Scooter," she said. "Come here to your mother."

I hadn't heard the nickname in so long, I nearly didn't respond. In fact, it wasn't the name at all, but her faint smile that drew me slowly to her. I placed one foot in front of the other, as if weighed down by an impossibly heavy backpack.

"Ralph," my mother said. "Bless your hearts, both of you."

CHAPTER 69

JAMES PAID SIX HUNDRED DOLLARS TO SOME middle schooler he found through a website for a tutorial on how to open a back door into the database software used by 92 percent of private healthcare facilities. Six hundred wasted dollars if the Gadwall Specialist Center used another brand.

Having arrived by sailboat, captained and owned by Lexie, James and Sherlock entered the center through the dock doorway Ralph had left open. They wore clear-glass eye safety glasses, black baseball caps pulled down low, blue jeans, and navy blue T-shirts that read on the back:

NETWORK NERDS

CONNECT WITH US

They separated in search of a utility room or wall box containing the center's local area networking, internet, and Ethernet connections.

Sherlock found a promising candidate: a door marked "Authorized Use Only." The building's computer and telephone wires ran through the basement hallway atop an overhead wire channel. Nearly all the blue networking wires headed through a hole into that room.

It took Sherlock seven minutes to pick the door's lock.

"If you take any longer, I'm going to have a nap," James complained.

"You want to try?" Sherlock showed James the three needle-like tools he was manipulating to pick the lock.

"Shut up."

"Wake up your laptop," Sherlock advised, "and be ready. It's my fault this has taken so long, but it's going to be yours if we're caught."

Hugging a mother I thought I'd lost long ago was one of the greatest moments ever. I sensed her reluctance. It felt like she considered me too fragile to hug. Like she might break me. Maybe she'd been away from kids for too long. That made my throat catch.

I was a softy.

"We're going now, Mrs. M," Ralph said. "Moria has some coveralls and a hat for you. Why don't you carry some of your art supplies? Moria and I will get that chair in the corner." He turned around so she could get dressed. I helped her. That was the second-best moment ever. We'd guessed at a pair of Hippo Movers coveralls a size too big, but it actually helped make her look different. All we had to do was get to the freight elevator unquestioned.

The fifty or sixty feet suddenly seemed like miles.

We packed up her easel and some of her paint supplies along with a small pile of her favorite watercolors. Ralph and I figured out a way to carry the stuffed chair so he didn't have to use his bad arm and I didn't get squished like a bug—we turned it on its side and slid it on the floor on one of its arms.

The three of us made it out of the room and

into the hall without being noticed. But it didn't last.

"Hello?" A woman's voice from behind us.

Ralph turned. I grabbed Mother before she showed her face.

"Hippo Moving," Ralph said to the woman. A nurse, I realized, catching her uniform in a convex corridor mirror mounted high in the corner of the hallway.

"What have we here? Someone leaving us?"

Mother tried to turn again. Again, I stopped her.

Panic time. Ralph couldn't mention Mother's room. He had to name a patient's room that belonged to someone who might be leaving the facility. But Ralph was smarter than most.

"Not moving out, miss. Replacing a chair with a new one." He made his voice amusing. "We'll take any work we can get. Ours is a family business." In one quick explanation, Ralph had informed our adversary of what we were up to, and why it would take three people including a pint-sized girl like me to move a single chair.

"Always like to see things freshened up," the nurse said. She continued forward to walk past us. I had the sickening feeling she wanted a look at me and Mother but without making a big deal about it.

I hated myself for pulling a stunt on Mother, but the stakes were too high. I did that trick of kneeing her in the back of her own knee. Her leg unlocked and she folded forward and I caught her just as the nurse passed. There was no way the nurse could have seen Mother's face.

Ralph looked at me with something approaching admiration as Mother recovered and the nurse left us behind. We reached and entered the elevator.

Now came the hard part.

CHAPTER 70

"WHAT IS THIS?" SHERLOCK ASKED JAMES, who sat on the floor with his laptop plugged into a blue Ethernet wire.

"I thought you knew everything."

"I find what you're doing intriguing," Sherlock said.

"Another few strokes, and the system will say that Mother was officially released today."

"Then it gets tricky," Sherlock said.

"Yeah, well, there is that. You're the one who thought it up. *And*, how to pull it off."

"Putting a new patient into the system has to be authorized by—"

"A specific doctor. Yeah, I get that. You've said it ten times."

"Four."

"Shut up."

"A doctor on duty."

"That makes five."

"Very funny," Sherlock said.

"She's never going to talk to you again, you know?"

The computer room was kept unreasonably cold to protect the machines from overheating. Sherlock found the low hum annoying. He kept quiet.

"Bum sauce, Sherlost, but it's the truth."

"Truth does not have a present and a past, a beginning or end. Your sister and I have both."

"I'm talking about the end. Moria's done with you."

Sherlock found the cold penetrating as well.

"Get this done, man!"

"No problem. A few more clicks and Lois is going to find herself in Mother's situation. Fair is fair." James clicked the computer's trackpad and began to giggle. It was an evil giggle Sherlock had never heard from him before.

Ralph and I put Mother into the sailboat's cabin. Lexie helped us get her down the steep steps. Mother's eyes flared. This was all too much for her.

"Someday, Mother, I'll introduce you to a boy named Sherlock. I hate him. He's an oaf. But he has his good points. This whole thing's his plan. It's brilliant, of course, because that's just the kind of boy he is. He calls it 'ironic,' which is fine, I suppose, so long as one understands irony. Personally, I find it a little tricky."

"I don't understand." Mother sounded as if she might cry.

"We're going to help you with that, Mrs. M.," Ralph said. "For now, we need you to trust us."

Mother nodded grimly.

A few minutes later, Ralph and I reached the van. We helped the semiconscious Lois to her feet, careful not to bang her head.

CHAPTER 71

At 4:17 that same afternoon, a pharmacy tech named Marvin Hoshcenfelt was making the rounds on the second floor of the Gadwall Specialist Center. He knocked and opened the door to room 224.

Glancing at his electronic tablet, Marvin matched the patient's face with her record on file. The patient was too groggy to say hello, which only made sense given the strength of the sleeping pill that had been prescribed by the admitting doctor, Dr. Kamat. The patient was scheduled to receive the medication for the following three days. What amounted to something close to a "chemically induced coma," sometimes used on those patients who needed extra rest at the start of their stays.

Marvin checked the patient for her wristband and found it missing.

"What have you done with it?" he asked the woman, knowing she was too far gone to answer.

He checked under the bed. In the sheets. In the crack at the head of the bed. Nowhere to be found.

Wasn't the first time a patient had managed to cut one off a wrist, though it wasn't the easiest thing to do.

"We'll get you set up with a new one," he told the silent woman. "Never you mind about it."

He helped her sit up and swallow the two pills she was scheduled to take.

He lay her back down, making sure her head looked comfortable on the pillow.

Marvin moved over to and opened the door.

"Goodnight, Lois. See you tomorrow."

CHAPTER 72

FRIENDS ARE HARD TO MAKE AND EASY TO LOSE. It's even more true, more painful when the friend is treasured.

Brothers were never meant to be friends. I was lucky I'd managed it for a while. But I wasn't sure that friendship would ever return after everything that had happened.

Summer school ended without ceremony. The last three weeks were painfully boring. I woke up every morning wishing I were somewhere else. The idea that James was connected to people like Hildebrandt showed me how insane my brother had become. Baskerville Academy had been—was!—the worst thing for him ever. He was nothing short of a criminal, and a good one at that. He'd be fifteen in a few weeks—I wasn't sure I'd ever know him better than I did right now, and that made me infinitely sad.

Mother and Ralph picked me up when the blessed day at the end of the term arrived. James was staying a few extra days. I didn't want to know what that was about.

"You look better already," I said, sharing the backseat of the town car with her.

"Thank you, Moria." Mother's voice wasn't used to speaking, even now.

"How are you? Do you like . . . you know . . . being home?"

Only then did I realize she was wearing all black. That pretty much told me all I had to know about how she'd taken losing Father.

Ralph caught me in the car's mirror. His eyes said, *Don't go there.*

Please remember, I was twelve.

"From what I know, Mother, Father did everything he could to protect you. From people who might have tried to hurt you in order to get at him."

Mother looked out the side window. "There must be a million colors of green out there."

"I suppose," I said. Had she heard me? I wondered.

"Your father enjoyed autumn most of all."

She sounded about five years old. Her recovery was going to take time. She'd been in that little room too long. I felt like crying. But I was done crying. I was done wishing for things.

But not dreaming. I would never give up dreaming.

"Maybe we could go to the Cape for Labor Day," I proposed. Sherlock would be working. "James, Ralph, you, me. There's this girl, Lexie, but I don't know if she'll come if James is there. I kind of think she might, though."

"The colors," she said. "The cool air. They appealed to him so very much."

"I'll bet," I said. I tried to win Ralph's eyes in the mirror, but he was driving now.

CHAPTER 73

I SMELLED MUFFINS. BLUEBERRY. THERE WAS something about the Cape house that made every scent special. Coffee. Bacon. Blueberry muffins.

The morning sun shone so brightly through my windows that I went over to turn the little spindle that narrowed the slats of the blinds.

There was a sailboat out there. A sloop. Gorgeous thing. Maybe a half mile off shore, its sails luffing.

Something was unfastened from the bow and put over the side. It looked like a Sunfish sailboat or maybe a Sailfish. Turned out to be a paddleboard.

A figure stood atop it, working the long paddle, alternating sides.

I dug around looking for my binoculars, usually used to search for whales or identify large birds.

James. He wore colorful Hawaiian jams, an orange Burton T-shirt, and a dark tan he hadn't had the last time I'd seen him.

The sails snapped with the wind. The sailboat headed southeast in the direction of Woods Hole or maybe the Vineyard.

James paddled for shore, some white seagulls finding him and playing just overhead.

I didn't know the boy—my brother!—as well as I once had. But I wanted to. I hoped he'd let me in. Like with Mother's recovery, I was prepared to give it time.

Mother walked out onto the grass, shielding her eyes. I joined her.

James paddled closer.

I found a smile.

CHAPTER 74

FORMER FBI DIRECTOR CONNECTED TO DECADES–OLD ROBBERY

Tanner Walters with Rob Barry

The Suffolk County Attorney General has confirmed a joint investigation with the Justice Department into former FBI Director Mathias Hildebrandt's alleged participation in an armored car robbery after a witness came forward offering to testify to events surrounding the more than fifty-year-old crime.

The 1.4-million-dollar robbery of an armored car took place on Route 6 near West Dennis. The money was never recovered. A security guard, Harold Colletti, died of gunshot wounds at the scene. The murder weapon had remained missing until its unexplained appearance at the Cobb Street precinct on August 19 of this year. Sources close to the investigation confirm Hildebrandt is being sought for questioning. No charges have been made.

Hildebrandt, who served as a distinguished FBI Director for twenty-two years, could not be reached for comment.

James folded the newspaper and smiled smugly. He reached for a glass of orange juice, noting the two empty places at the breakfast table set for me and Mother. We needed our beauty rest.

"Everything OK, James?" Ralph delivered a plate of steaming eggs one-handed.

"Better than ever. We've got him now, Ralph.

Off the Directory for good, but still working to achieve his plan."

"It won't be without repercussions," Ralph said. "Your going against your father's wishes takes the Scowerers down a dangerous path."

"So you've already told me. I'm in charge now, Ralph. Father didn't understand the global economy," James said.

"I mean no offense, but you're fourteen."

"At thirteen, a kid named Jordan Romero climbed Everest. Nadia Comăneci won a gold medal in gymnastics. Mozart was having an opera performed."

"And you?" Ralph said.

"Conniving crook? Creative criminal? World's greatest criminal mastermind? You tell me."

"World's most arrogant kid?" I said, from the doorway.

"That, too," James said, motioning to an empty place setting.

"You broke Lexie's heart, you know?" I said, sitting down. I poured myself orange juice.

"I know," he said, his voice softening.

"Yours too?" I asked.

Ralph took the opportunity to retreat into the kitchen.

"I don't have a heart, remember?" James said.

"I can help you find it again," I said. "If you'll let me."

"Hide-and-seek?" James said, trying for a joke. And failing.

"Something like that."

"What if I'm a lost cause?"

I considered that long and hard. His endless confrontations with Sherlock. His dismissal of me. Of Lexie. His clinging to his thugs and his Scowerers.

"Then heaven help us," I said.

James smirked, scrambled eggs bulging his cheeks.

"Heaven help us all."

READ THEM ALL!